MURDER SQUAD

MURDER SQUAD

Edited by Martin Edwards

Foreword by Val McDermid

FLAMBARD

First published in England in 2001 by Flambard Press
Stable Cottage, East Fourstones, Hexham NE47 5DX

Typeset by Barbara Sumner
Cover design by Gainford Design Associates
Front cover photograph by Sally Mundy
Printed in England by Cromwell Press, Trowbridge, Wiltshire

A CIP catalogue record for this book
is available from the British Library.
ISBN 1 873226 51 9

Flambard Press wishes to thank Northern Arts
for its financial support.

northern
arts

Contents

Acknowledgements

John Baker's 'Defence' was first published in *Fresh Blood 2*, ed. Mike Ripley and Maxim Jakubowski (The Do-Not Press, 1997); Chaz Brenchley's 'Up the Airy Mountain' in *Crimewave 3*, *Burning Down the House*, ed. Andy Cox (TTA Press, 2000); and Cath Staincliffe's 'Rock-A-Bye-Baby' in *Shots*, vol. 3, no. 9 (Spring 2001).

The publishers of the books from which extracts are taken for the Collage are:
City Life and Penguin, *The City Life Book of Manchester Short Stories* (Cath Staincliffe)
Victor Gollancz, *Death Minus Zero* and *King of the Streets* (both John Baker)
Headline, *The Mushroom Man* and *Some by Fire* (both Stuart Pawson), *Dead Wrong* and *Go Not Gently* (both Cath Staincliffe)
Hodder & Stoughton, *The Samaritan* (Chaz Brenchley), *First Cut Is the Deepest* (Martin Edwards)
Macmillan, *The Baby Snatcher* and *The Crow Trap* (both Ann Cleeves), *Caging the Tiger*, *Dying Embers* and *Past Reason* (all Margaret Murphy)
Paitkus, *All the Lonely People* and *Eve of Destruction* (both Martin Edwards)

Val McDermid

FOREWORD

Somewhere between three and four hundred crime novels are published every year. Although there is an eager and voracious audience for the genre, very few of us can manage to read between six and eight books every week. So for all but a handful of bestselling authors whose publishers spend the promotional budget to ensure both sales and profile, the burning question becomes, 'How do I get my work noticed?'

The seven writers featured in this collection came up with the novel idea that strength lies in numbers and formed Murder Squad. Thanks to the social network of crime writers, they were already friends – all seven are familiar faces at the Northern Chapter gatherings of the Crime Writers' Association. But they took advantage of that social connection to forge a professional grouping aimed at bringing their work to a wider audience.

The group's members are available collectively, individually or in any combination to grace literary festivals, library events, bookshop readings, post-prandial speeches or murder-mystery evenings. Knowing them as I do, I suspect they'd probably come up with a more than adequate cabaret for any occasion from a christening to a wake. And this anthology amply demonstrates that the whole is indeed greater than the sum of its parts. Murder Squad's members are a rainbow coalition, spanning among them the whole colourful spectrum of contemporary British crime ficiton.

For this genre is no longer the either/or of police procedural or village mystery that used to typify British crime writing, and its range is exhibited here. The seven authors take the opportunity to reveal that they're no one-trick ponies. History mystery is represented, the time periods ranging from Martin Edwards's study of power in medieval Wales, to 1960s America, via John Baker's creepy Victorian Cornish gothic. Psychological terror has its place, with nail-biting contributions from Cath Staincliffe, Margaret Murphy and Ann Cleeves. There are twists in the tail from Chaz Brenchley, Stuart Pawson, Ann Cleeves and John Baker. And both Margaret and Stuart remind us that humour is alive and well among the corpses. Victims take revenge, killers are caught on the hooks of their own cleverness; there are bluffs, double-bluffs and even triple-bluffs alongside the double-crosses and sleight-of-hand misdirections.

The short story is a notoriously difficult form to work with, placing enormous constraints on the writer. It is far, far more than a clever little idea with a sting in the tale. Characters must be delineated in the most economic of ways, just as the finest cartoonists can summon up the essence of a public figure in a few telling lines. The story itself must be simple enough to be unfolded in a few short pages, and yet it must also be sufficiently intriguing to attract and hold the reader's attention. There is no room for languid exposition, yet there must also be a vivid thumbnail picture that sets the story in time and space.

Set against this benchmark, the stories in this anthology acquit themselves well. It's all the more creditable since, with the exception of the prolific Chaz Brenchley, none of these novelists has published many short stories. What has been for me the most pleasant surprise is to see how writers of series have spread their wings and tried for something very different from their usual style and tone.

So we have Cath Staincliffe writing a heartbreaking, insightful story from the point of view of a mentally disturbed woman, as well as giving us a miniature adventure from her usual protagonist, Sal Kilkenny. We find Stuart Pawson venturing into the dark world of the serial killer as well as showing us a more depressing episode than usual from the career of his regular cop, Charlie Priest. Martin Edwards abandons altogether his usual protagonist, lawyer Harry Devlin, to demonstrate that he has a ventriloquist's gift for other people's voices.

This collection is a showcase of some of the most interesting voices in contemporary British crime fiction. These are all writers who constantly strive to improve their grasp of their craft and who are never satisfied with leaving the genre as they found it.

Murder Squad is not a gimmick. It's a genuine attempt to demonstrate the diversity and the quality of what is being produced by writers who are shelved under crime by booksellers and librarians. Play your cards right, and they'll be coming to a venue near you. This book is a celebration. So sit yourself down with a glass or a steaming mug of what you fancy, and indulge yourself.

Or else.

Martin Edwards

INTRODUCTION

Welcome to *Murder Squad* – crime fiction to die for! This book represents something new in crime fiction. It is the first anthology to have been put together by a 'virtual collective' of established crime writers, who have teamed together to seek an even wider audience for their work.

Margaret Murphy told the story of the creation of Murder Squad in an essay which attracted considerable attention and went on to win the Crime Writers' Association's Leo Harris Award:

> The idea originated when, discouraged and demoralised by being told that my good reviews didn't translate into sales figures, I decided to try to find a way of building my profile. I approached John Baker, Chaz Brenchley, Ann Cleeves, Martin Edwards, Stuart Pawson and Cath Staincliffe, who all readily agreed to take part in the venture. We decided initially that we would design and have printed a brochure advertising our books and our various talents, aimed principally at booksellers and libraries. We narrowed down the services we were prepared to offer to readings, signings, workshops and masterclasses, discussion panels, projects, residencies and talks.

Not too narrow a range of services, then!

The Squad was launched in the spring of 2000 at a bookshop event to celebrate the opening day of a new branch of Borders on the Wirral, and from that day it has gone from strength to strength. Because the seven of us are scattered far and wide across the North of England, we communicate mainly by email – pretty much every day. Technology plays a vital part in our activities, not least because of our website, masterminded by John Baker, whose cool expertise in matters technical always leaves me in awe. The site is interactive and, although we have from the first circulated a free news bulletin to readers, we now focus mainly on emailing our newsletter to people who wish to keep up to date with our recent activities and forthcoming exploits. We hope that everyone who enjoys this book will feel moved to get in touch with us and subscribe to the complimentary newsletter service.

We have a busy calendar of events, updated regularly, which can be viewed at the site: www.murdersquad.co.uk. Apart from bookshop and library gigs (some of which feature Ann Cleeves's much-acclaimed 'Body in the Library' production), we appear regularly at literary and arts festivals up and down the country. Although we all live in the North of England – in fact, we all first met at meetings of the Northern Chapter of the Crime Writers' Association – our activities span the whole country: you are as likely to find us appearing in Plymouth as in Pontefract. We don't see ourselves as regional writers, but rather as authors whose books, albeit often set in the North, have something to say which will appeal to readers wherever they are based. With that in mind, we are at the time of writing planning to venture further afield – initially to Europe (several of us are published in various countries on the Continent) and eventually to the United States.

All this activity takes time and, although it is a great deal of fun, we know that we mustn't forget that what brought us together in the first place is crime writing. So what better than to put together a selection of fresh work in the form of a crime anthology? This book is much more than a sampler of our current writing. We have sought to stretch our talents and, in many cases, to try something quite different from our usual stories. So there are rare short-story outings for Stuart Pawson's Charlie Priest and Cath Staincliffe's Sal Kilkenny, while John Baker, Ann Cleeves and I have forsaken our series sleuths altogether – if only temporarily – to contribute stand-alone tales. Margaret Murphy seldom writes short stories, but displays here a real talent for the form, while Chaz Brenchley shows again that he has few equals in the field of cutting-edge crime. The book also includes 'something completely different' – an edited version of a collage of our writing which we performed at crimefests up and down the country during the Squad's first year of existence. The collage was received wonderfully well and its appearance in book form is, as far as I know, a first in crime publishing. We hope that readers who have not previously encountered our work will be encouraged to seek out the rest of it, and that those who are familiar with the books of one or two of us will take a closer look at what the other contributors can do at novel length.

A few words of thanks. Peter and Margaret Lewis of Flambard Press are more than first-class publishers: they have been good friends to all seven of us. We are also indebted to Val McDermid, one of the world's leading crime novelists, for sparing the time in a hectic schedule to contribute a most generous Foreword. We are grateful to our families who put up with us, somehow, despite all the demands and ups-and-downs of the writing life. And finally, a word of thanks to our readers. We depend on you and we hope this book gives you as much pleasure to read as it gave us to write. And if it does – you will tell your friends about us, won't you?

Ann Cleeves

THE PLATER

The land was east-coast flat, washed by floods, so the ditches were full and the fields on either side of him greener than he could remember. It was a familiar road, long and straight and narrow. He'd picked up the Saab in Hull that afternoon and now he was on his way home. He'd spend the night at the cottage before delivering the car to a showroom in Coventry early the next day. He liked his own bed; it was better than sleeping in the vehicle or a cheap B and B and it didn't add much to the mileage. From Coventry he'd hitch-hike to Bristol, taking his trade plates with him, and collect an Audi for Liverpool. That's what he did for a living; he drove other people's cars from one end of the country to another.

It was July and hot. The ditches steamed as the water evaporated, and the road disappeared into a heat haze before it turned a corner so it seemed to go on for ever, straight and flat to the horizon. Way ahead of him was a small, squat bus, but there was no other traffic. The verges on each side of the road were lush and untreated. Reeds in the dykes and cow parsley so tall that it formed a hedge. He drove slowly. There was no rush. Since he'd lost Suzy there was nothing to hurry home to.

Ahead of him a small drama was being played out. The bus slowed to a stop and a couple of schoolkids jumped off. Lads with shirts hanging out and scruffy sports bags. As they chased up a farm track a woman appeared. The plater thought she must have come from one of the tarted-up cottages set back from the road, but the bright afternoon sun shone straight into his eyes and he couldn't be certain. Suddenly she was there, a black, mad silhouette, running and waving after the bus. It was clear to the plater that the driver hadn't seen her. He indicated and drove on. She stood for a moment looking after the bus, as if she could drag it back towards her, just with the power of her will. Then she gave up. In a single gesture of defiance she turned to face the on-coming traffic, planted one foot firmly ahead of her, and stuck out her thumb.

He would always stop for other platers. That went without saying. A rule as fixed as his contract with the agency. He needed the others to get him home on the dark, wet nights when he stood at motorway junctions, just as they needed him. But he never picked up anyone else. The students and the soldiers on leave and the motorists who'd broken down could find their own way home. He hated making conversation. He'd chosen this job because it had given him the chance to be on his own.

But this time he stopped. He was drugged by the heat and the sun in his eyes, and something of this woman reminded him of Suzy. Besides, he seemed to have no choice in the matter. Although he had already driven past her he stopped and reversed. For the first time he saw her clearly. She was older than Suzy, at least ten years older, smaller, more delicate. Her hair was fine as rabbit fur, faded blond, pinned up with a tortoise shell comb so her neck seemed long and thin enough for him to put one hand round. Her brown eyes had sparks in them. He leant across the passenger seat and opened the car door for her. Until then she'd made no move to get in.

'Where are you going?' he asked.

'Town?' A question. Or a riddle. Surely she knew where she wanted to be.

It was further than he'd intended taking her, past where he lived, but he nodded. When he'd opened the door he'd smelled the humid air – a mixture of cows and ditchwater – and then her perfume.

She got in quickly as if she were worried that he'd change his mind. Or that she'd change hers. She was wearing sandals and a blue, sleeveless dress printed with silver stars. There was pink polish on her toe nails, a scattering of freckles on her shoulder. The dress rode up when she stepped in and her leg was brown and smooth. No freckles there. She was clutching a bag made of purple velvet patchwork on her lap. It would have been big enough to contain everything *he* needed for an overnight stay, including a lightweight sleeping bag and a couple of maps. But he didn't think it would do for a woman. Even Suzy had needed a rucksack when she went on the road. The smallness of the bag confused him. He didn't understand what she intended. If she was planning to go all the way into the big town she wouldn't be back before nightfall. She seemed to have left home in a hurry, without any thought.

'God,' she said. She shifted her hips so she was comfortable in the leather seat, lifting her buttocks and pulling down the dress. 'It was never that easy when I was young.'

He stared at her but she didn't move again.

'Hitching, I mean. I thought I wouldn't stand a chance at my age.'

'Aren't you worried?' he asked slowly. 'Hitch-hiking on your own?'

'It's not something I do every day. The last time was when I was a student. Twenty years ago. And the rest! But when the bus drove off I thought *Sod it. Why not?*'

'I saw you think that. That was why I stopped.'

She turned and looked at him. 'Did you? How very percep-tive.'

He could feel his face prickle with a blush so he put the Saab into gear and pulled off. Still there were no other cars.

'I'm running away,' she announced. Her voice wasn't loud but it was clear. If you were at one end of a church and she was at the other, and she whispered, you'd still hear every word. He wondered what had made him think of churches because he hadn't been inside one since Suzy's funeral, and that was a whole year before, almost to the day. He allowed himself to take his eyes off the road for a moment to look at his passenger. Was she serious? He suspected she was laughing at him. Under the clear voice, he thought he heard laughter.

Then she did give a little chuckle out loud. 'I'm running away from my husband. He'll come home from work and no one will be there. No one to pour him a drink or cook his dinner.'

He didn't say anything.

'You're shocked.'

'No.' Of course he was and she could tell.

'Perhaps you think you should drive me straight back.'

'Only if you want me to.' Part of him had wanted her to say yes. He was already regretting the impulse to stop. No more complications, he'd told himself after Suzy. But trapped by the car her perfume was stronger, heady. She played with the velvet of her bag, squeezing it into pleats with long, supple fingers.

'No,' she said. 'Really, I don't.' More gently she added, 'I'll probably only run away for one day. Teach him not to take me for granted. Tomorrow I'll go back and cook the supper like a good little wife.'

It occurred to him then that perhaps Suzy had only meant to run away for one day and that she'd intended to come back to him. The thought winded him as if he'd been kicked in the chest. He fought for breath. The woman seemed not to notice his distress.

'One day of adventure,' she was saying. 'Time out. That's all I want.'

A tractor and trailer pulled out of a lane in front of him. He overtook it smoothly.

'What's your name?' he demanded. The question was too abrupt. He could hear that as soon as the words were spoken. The image of Suzy as she might have been, apologetic on the doorstep, stopped him thinking straight.

'Belle.'

16

'I had a girlfriend called Suzy.' Why had he told her that? Conversation didn't work this way. He'd got it wrong again. You had to talk about things no one cared about, at first at least. And anyway it was dangerous to bring up the subject of Suzy. He wasn't sure he could remember the story.

The woman seemed not to notice he'd broken the rules. 'Did you? What happened to her?'

'She walked out one night.'

'Like me,' Belle said.

'But she never came back.'

'Oh,' she said in the whisper which would fill a church. 'I'm sorry. That's so sad.'

He looked at her again, expecting to find her mocking him, the smirk, the 'isn't he dumb?' pity he usually provoked. But she seemed moved by his loneliness. He thought she understood it. Perhaps she wasn't being frivolous in running away. Perhaps she didn't have a marriage worth saving. She touched his arm, a gesture of sympathy, and there was a sort of dreaminess in her eyes. He wondered fleetingly if he might feature in her adventure. He might make it more special for her.

'Town then, yeah?' He tried to keep his voice natural, though a croak had developed. He wished he was wearing something different. Not the jeans he'd bought in the market for a fiver and the checked shirt with the frayed collar. He wished he'd had a shower before leaving home.

'Why?' she asked. 'Where were *you* going?'

'Home.' The other words came as a mumbled rush. 'You could come if you like. I could make you some tea. I've got herbal. I'll take you into town later.' Suzy had liked herbal. It would still be alright, wouldn't it, wrapped up in its foil packet, even after a year? As he waited for the woman to reply he felt as if he were growing, that his limbs were getting longer and more awkward and clumsy, that he was taking up so much space in the car that there was no air left for either of them to breathe.

17

She hesitated and he knew she was thinking of her young days, when she'd taken risks, gone hitching on her own and talked to strangers. He realised that was what he'd been banking on: her leaving her middle-aged wifely caution behind.

'Herbal tea,' she said gently. 'Why not?'

So he looked in his mirror to check the road was empty, and indicated and turned into the track.

Belle *adored* the cottage. That was what she said when she first saw it. He'd known that she'd like it. Suzy had been hooked by it too when she'd first wandered up the track. 'Wow,' she'd said. 'It's, like, really fairy tale. Hansel and Gretel.' Love at first sight.

It was made of old brick and flint. A red-tiled roof which came so low that he could easily reach the black, cast-iron gutter with his hand. Outside, a saw-horse and a pile of logs, a couple of feral hens, a place to park his cars. Inside, four rooms, unchanged pretty much since his mother's day, but tidy. He didn't like clutter. And a neat extension that he'd built on the back. He didn't invite Belle inside. Not yet, he thought. He'd have to be careful with her. They stood for a moment looking at the house. The low sun threw their shadows ahead of them. His seemed enormous in comparison with hers. Not Hansel and Gretel, he thought. Some other story.

'But it's magic,' Belle said. 'It can't have changed for a hundred years.'

'Of course it's changed.' He spoke more sharply than he'd intended but he felt defensive. 'There's a bathroom now. Suzy needed a bathroom.' He wanted to explain what a job that had been, the cesspit and the plumbing, but thought better of it. 'And there's a phone. I need a phone for work.'

'It's not just the building,' Belle said. 'It's the quiet.' He listened to sounds he didn't usually hear. Water in the field drain. The sandpaper scratching of a hen. A wood pigeon. She shut her eyes and he saw a spider's web of fine lines around them. As he watched, the lids lifted and she looked out past the row of coppiced willow to where cows grazed. The quiet had bothered Suzy in the end, but it seemed not to trouble Belle.

'Tell me about your work.' She turned and smiled at him. He felt faint again like when he'd first smelled her, and stood up to compose himself.

'I'll make the tea first. That'll be best.'

It had been sunny when Suzy had arrived, but that had been a winter late-afternoon sun in a pink and grey sky, with a frost starting to form. He'd been out to fetch logs and she'd appeared at the end of the track. He'd stopped, still bent over the barrow, and watched her come closer. She'd been dressed in black leather and carried a crash helmet under her arm, and he was reminded of a film about aliens in space suits. It was *that* strange to see anyone there. But she was on her own and there wasn't a flying saucer in sight. He'd straightened as she came up to him.

'Can I use your phone?' she'd said. 'I came off my bike. Frozen surface water. The road's dead greasy' But she wasn't looking at him. She was looking at the cottage, grey now that the sun had gone, icicles hanging from the eaves. That's when she made the comment about the fairy tale.

He'd invited Suzy in immediately because he couldn't keep her outside when it was freezing, and that was what she was there for, to use the phone. She'd reminded him of that as he stood holding the rubber grips of the wheelbarrow, staring at her. 'You do have a phone?' Stamping her fat leather boots up and down to tell him how cold she was. And besides, she was different from Belle, more confident, with her curious eyes and her voice demanding attention and answers.

He would have been shy in a stranger's house, but Suzy had wandered through it touching and probing, running her finger over the back of the chair where he sat in the evening, making him open the little gate in the bottom of the range to show where the fuel went, picking up a teacup to look at the pattern on the side.

'Is it just you here?'

'Since mother died.'

'Don't you mind being on your own?'

'Sometimes…' he'd hesitated. '… Sometimes I'd prefer the company.'

The next day she'd turned up with her stuff. He'd heard the motorbike coming down the track, so loud he could feel the vibrations through his feet and it was as if the foundations were shaking. It seemed she'd had a row with her boyfriend. She described it but the plater wasn't listening.

'You don't mind?' she asked. A challenge. 'I mean, you did sort of say…'

He hadn't been able to speak, dizzy with disbelief and delicious indecision. She'd stood on the square of carpet in the parlour. 'Of course I'll need a bathroom.' And softened the demand by taking his hand and tilting her head and standing on her toes to push her tongue between his lips. Then stroking his hair in a way that was almost tender. By then the indecision was over. He had no choice.

'Tell me about your work,' Belle said again, and he left winter behind and returned to the smells and the sounds of a July afternoon. She was sitting on a wooden bench set along the front wall of the house. One of the smells was of roasting wood preservative. He'd made the tea and put it on the bench beside her, then sat on the grass, not wanting to crowd her. He knew his size sometimes intimidated. She'd wanted to bring out the tray but he was still reluctant to let her into the house. If he'd left Suzy outside that first time, offered to make the phone call on her behalf, he wouldn't have this guilt which he carried round in his gut like a permanent bellyache. He tried to push Suzy out of his head but it was difficult because, despite their physical differences, the women had become blurred in his mind. Perhaps he'd been more upset than he'd realised by the anniversary of Suzy's death.

He saw that Belle was waiting for him to answer. He stumbled into an explanation of what it was to be a plater.

'Do you enjoy it?'

'Oh yes,' he said. 'It's the cars. How could I drive a car like that otherwise? And it's the maps too. You move across the map in a different line each day.' He stopped, realising he was using almost exactly the same words as when he'd first described his work to Suzy.

'I've seen the platers,' Belle said. 'Men at motorway junctions carrying trade plates? They must have been. I didn't know what they were doing. You don't really take any notice do you? They all seem to look the same.' She was excited. It was as if she seldom came across a subject she knew nothing about. 'And so organised... It is a man thing, I suppose. Not really a suitable job for a woman.'

'There was one woman.'

'Was there?' Excited again. A pause, a flash of inspiration. 'Not Suzy?'

How could she have guessed? 'She enjoyed coming out with me,' he said slowly.

'She would. Of course.' Belle was looking out beyond the cows to the horizon. He waited for her to go on but she seemed lost in thought.

'At first that was enough. She loved the fast cars. She was wild about speed. I drove too fast for her because that was what she wanted. She sat beside me. Shouting "Faster. Faster." Like a kid on a ride at the fair. But it couldn't have been enough. Without telling me she contacted the agency. She fixed the insurance and the contract. Without telling me.' His voice sounded too loud, a sort of booming in his ears, and he tried to control it, to become reasonable. He didn't want to scare Belle away. 'I came in one night and she wasn't there. She'd left a note. She was delivering a VW to Wolverhampton and bringing back a People Carrier. Working as a plater. I lay awake, listening for the engine, watching for the headlights on the bedroom ceiling. When she got in she said I was daft for being anxious.'

'Perhaps she felt trapped,' Belle said. 'She wanted her own life.'

'Her own life?' he demanded. 'What does that mean? It wasn't safe, what she was doing. My nerves were ragged with waiting for her night after night. And all the time I was working I was wondering where she was. In the end I told her: "If you work as a plater, you don't live here."'

'So she went?'

'She packed up her clothes and left while I was at work.' He hesitated. He didn't know how much more to say. But it was a story and stories needed endings. 'Two days later the police were here. Two of them. A grey-haired bloke and a girl so young she looked as though she should still be at school. I'd heard their car and I'd thought it might be Suzy, so it threw me, seeing the uniforms standing there. She was dead. Hit and run. She'd been hitching on the motorway. I'd always said she should get the train once she'd delivered the car…' He'd told it well, he thought. Well enough.

Belle touched his hand and squeezed it gently a couple of times, as she'd squeezed the velvet bag when she was sitting in his car.

'You can't blame yourself.'

'No? Maybe not.'

'Did they ever find the driver?'

The guilt got him again, weighed him down so it was a struggle to stand up. 'No,' he said. 'They never found out who did it.' He remembered the police officers, standing on the doorstep, looking round the yard for a car which had already been delivered to Stamford.

Now he was on his feet, looking down at the top of her head. He saw the stray hairs escaping from the comb, the long swan's neck 'Look,' he said. 'Why don't you come inside?'

*

The next day the plater drove the Saab to Coventry, then stopped for an early lunch at a transport café close to the M4. Not part of the usual routine but the weather had changed. There was a blustery west wind and sudden squally showers. The café was an ugly house built of raw yellow brick with a concrete pull-in where trucks stopped overnight. Inside, it was all smoke and steam and the smell of fried food. Condensation ran in streams down the window. Someone had left a paper open with the mucky pots on the only empty table. The plater began to read.

The article, on an inside page, was about the search for a woman. She had last been seen by two schoolboys running for a bus on a country road. After that, it seemed, she'd disappeared. The police were anxious to trace her. Early the previous evening a neighbour had discovered the body of her husband in the cottage where they'd lived. The man had been strangled and by implication the woman was prime suspect in a murder enquiry. There was a photograph, which the plater studied carefully, even holding it up towards the flickering strip light, but it was grainy and blurred. It could have been of any middle-aged woman.

Belle folded the newspaper carefully, ran her finger along to straighten the crease and felt a stab of injured pride. She would have liked to tell the lorry drivers slumped over their sweet teas and ketchup-splattered chips. To shout her cleverness out loud. Not one murder. Two. Thanks to the plater she'd disappeared, become invisible, nothing but a woollen hat and a waterproof coat.

And no one would find his body for months. Who ever went to his cottage? Who cared about him? Not the agency when she'd phoned them and told them he didn't want to be considered for work for a while. Not after the Saab. The woman at the end of the phone had sounded relieved if anything. He would have been slow at the work and difficult to deal with. No loss.

Belle wiped the grease from her face with a paper handkerchief. The rain had stopped. She hoisted her velvet bag onto her shoulder, stuck the trade plates under her arm and made her way outside. She stood at the café entrance and stuck out her thumb. She only had to wait two minutes before a lorry pulled up.

Martin Edwards

ETERNALLY

Playing for time, I said, 'All that happened a long time ago.'

'I'd love you to tell me about it,' Alice said, putting down her notes and leaning over my bed.

Her perfume was discreet, the faintest hint of sandalwood. If only I were a few years younger. Well, quite a lot of years. I doubted if she was thirty-five and already she'd carved out separate reputations, first as an investigative journalist with *The Washington Post*, more recently as the author of a couple of bestsellers about Hollywood glitterati. She was shrewd and determined. Unwilling to take no for an answer. Exciting in any woman.

I started to cough. A passing nurse paused, but I nodded her away. Alice bent closer to me and I muttered, 'You don't want to listen to a sick old man, talking about the past.'

'It took me a long time to find you.' Wagging a slim finger. 'Hard work. At least the advance covered my flight to London.'

'Why bother? You can write your book without interviewing me.'

'I don't cut corners.' A sweet grin. 'Besides, I never shopped in Oxford Street before.'

'You haven't missed much.'

'Also, I'd like to hear what you have to say.'

I sucked in air: not as easy as it used to be. 'You said a few minutes ago that you just love a good murder mystery. But you're wrong. Max didn't kill his wife. Is that good enough for you?'

The corners of her mouth curved down. The crestfallen

expression made her look about nineteen; a man could easily be taken in by it and tell her more than it was safe to disclose.

'You were his friend, of course you believed in him. But even at the time, there was gossip. Rumours that the accident was too convenient.'

'Lorna was pretty and she died young. It's the stuff that myths are made of.' I made a show of stifling a yawn. 'If she'd been a little more talented, a little brighter, people would still remember her name.'

'Some people still do. That's why I have to mention her in my book.'

'There isn't a story. She had too much to drink one evening, fell down the stairs of their Long Island mansion and broke her pretty little neck.'

Alice touched my hand, grazing the palm with her nails. I felt her warm breath on my cheek. 'There is a story if her husband murdered her.'

'You haven't done your homework. Max was innocent. He spent the evening with us. He'd never have had time to get over to the house and kill Lorna.'

She didn't blink. 'Trust me. I always do my research very thoroughly.'

I burst into a racking cough and within a minute the nurse was pulling the curtains around my bed, shooing Alice away. I shut my eyes. I wasn't ready to step through death's door. I needed a little space, a little time, to decide what to say and do. Alice was so focused on making sure she got what she wanted.

In my mind, I saw Max again. A July afternoon in '68. The first time we had met since Lorna's death. He hadn't attended the funeral. Too sick, too eaten up with grief, so the story went. I sat in the front row at the church, not blinking, just remembering. There was an empty space beside me. Patty was still in shock after what had happened.

Max and I had been keeping our distance. He didn't call me,

I didn't call him. When I showed up at his apartment on East 61st Street, unable to stay away any longer, I was shocked by the change in him.

He still dressed like Joe College. Plaid pants, baggy crew-neck sweater, white socks and white US Keds. But his hair was different. Thick as ever, but with patches of grey that hadn't existed six months before. He kept glancing past me, as if any moment he expected Lorna's ghost to slink into the room.

'Thanks for coming,' he said.

A smell of burned toast hung in the air. At least it was better than cigarette smoke. The Colts and Packers were playing, but he switched off the set and started bustling in the kitchen. The refrigerator was packed to overflowing with lemons and Pepperidge Farm bread. He kept his gaze away from me as he threw raw eggs and coffee ice into the blender.

'How have you been?'

'Oh well, you know.'

Silly question. I suppose we both must have felt nervous. Were my hands shaking, or is that just an illusion of memory? I kept quiet while he made the coffee milkshake and fiddled with cheese and chopped liver for a Dagwood sandwich.

A baby Steinway sat in an alcove. On the shelves lay half a dozen score pads scooped together with rubber bands. I hazarded a guess that all of the pages were blank.

'Written anything lately?' I asked.

'Not a note,' he said. 'You?'

'Uh-uh.'

I sipped the milkshake. 'So you and Chrissie aren't writing together at present?'

He stared at me. 'I haven't seen Chrissie since Lorna died.'

'I see.'

'Do you?' His cheeks, pale until that moment, suffused with colour. 'I don't think so. Everyone believes that they see. Truth is, they see what they want to see. Something bad.'

I swallowed hard. 'Hey, I'm sorry I didn't get in touch.'

27

'Why should you have? I was the one who dumped on you. Found another lyricist.'

'I couldn't blame you. Chrissie's ten years younger and a thousand percent sexier than me.'

'What you aren't saying is, she never wrote a hit song in her life.'

I shrugged. 'Fashions change. The stuff we wrote, it doesn't make the charts any more. You were right, we needed a break from each other. Needed to freshen up.'

'Lorna hated me for it. She told me you were worth ten of Chrissie. She was right, but what the hell? Sorry, Steve.'

Awkwardly, he stretched out a hand and I shook it.

'People are whispering, aren't they?' he said quietly. Not meeting my eyes. Maybe he feared what he might see there.

'What do you mean?'

'C'mon, Steve. We've known each other a long time. We're old friends.'

'The best,' I said fervently. Despite everything, I meant it.

'Then tell me. Everyone thinks I killed Lorna, pushed her down those stairs. Isn't that the truth?'

'No.' The flat denial startled him, made him catch his breath. 'Okay, okay, there are one or two people who love to think the worst.'

'More than one or two. Chrissie's among them. As usual, she flatters herself.' He paused. 'She's stupid enough to believe I killed Lorna, just to be free for her.'

Next day, with Alice back at my bedside and fiddling with her tape recorder, I said, 'I'm not sure Max and I deserve a chapter in your book. We were never Goffin and King, or Leiber and Stoller.'

'You were different, you were a Brit.'

'Who married a girl from Greenwich Village.'

'She was a folk singer,' Alice said, as if I didn't know. 'How romantic.'

28

'And I was a lyricist whose sole claim to fame was the words to a Cliff Richard B-side. Patty and I met in a club in Soho at the end of the Fifties. I'd never met anyone quite like her. She was so lovely, so intense.'

'You wrote songs with her?'

'At first. Not a good idea, we both realised in the end. You can't work with someone you're passionate about. She was a wannabe Joan Baez, but my heart belonged to Tin Pan Alley. After I followed her to New York, I had a couple of breaks, grabbed a short-term contract with Famous Music. It went from there.'

A dreamy look came into her hazel eyes. 'What was it like in those days, working in the Brill Building?'

'One thing it wasn't, was glamorous. Eleven floors of offices and every one housed a music publisher. Each company had its writers' rooms, stuffy cubicles with just enough room for a beat-up piano and a couple of chairs. The windows didn't open, it was hell working with a guy like Max who smoked non-stop.' I coughed to make the point. 'I ought to sue, don't you think? That place surely killed me.'

'You all kept changing partners.'

'Sure. I'd write with one guy in the morning, another in the afternoon. That's the way it worked. But there was something about Max's melodies. They seemed to make a better fit with the words I wrote. Bobby Vinton liked our songs, Jay and the Americans gave us a Top Thirty hit. It went on from there. Before long the two of us were a team.'

'You met Lorna Key at recording session, so the story goes.'

'It's a true story,' I said. 'There was an Isley Brothers session and we had a song on the date. She was one of the girls singing in the background. You couldn't help but notice her. Even in pigtails and jeans, she was gorgeous. Her voice was raw, even as a kid she was a chain-smoker. Her lungs must have been in worse shape than Max's, but it wasn't her lungs that he was interested in. He said she had potential. Nice euphemism, huh?

He wanted her to start recording our demos. I went along with it, even though I never cared much for her sound. Subtlety was never her strong point.'

Alice glanced at her notebook. 'Soon she signed with Kapp Records.'

'Yeah, Lorna thought she'd become a star, but the truth is, Max pulled strings. They were married the week before her first single came out.'

'*Eternally.*'

Alice smiled and crooned the chorus.

> 'For as long as there's a deep blue sea,
> For as long as there's a you and me,
> I will love you eternally.'

I shifted under the bedclothes. 'I never claimed to be William Shakespeare.'

She glanced over her shoulder, caught the puzzled frown of the nurse walking into the ward. In the bed opposite, old Arthur gave a toothless grin and tried to mime applause with his wasted hands.

'It has a hook,' she said. 'I've been humming the blessed thing all day. Can't seem to get it out of my head.'

'Ah, the potency of cheap music.'

'Lorna's voice was stronger than mine.'

'She belted it out,' I agreed. 'Though that wasn't what it called for. *Eternally* is a tender love song. But Lorna, she didn't do tenderness. You talk about murder. Well, she murdered *Eternally*. It was always a favourite of mine. For once, the words came before the music. I'd written it for Patty, a token of our love.'

'I like the melody,' she said. Not altogether tactfully.

'Max was a smart writer. He'd switch time signatures, come up with ten and a half bar phrases, as if it was the most natural thing in the world. Lorna couldn't handle it. She'd stumble over the tricky bits, we did a dozen takes and then settled for the second. I thought it was lousy, kept asking how you can *rasp* a love song, but Max said it was wonderful.'

'He was besotted with her.'

'That's what people forget. And you know something? He was proved right. That song went straight into the charts at number twenty-nine. Almost made it to the top ten. Lorna Key never had a bigger record.'

'The publicity must have helped. Her marrying the composer.'

'Sure, the Press lapped it up.'

'Did you resent that? Max was always the one in the public eye, not you. Radio announcers used to talk about Max Heller songs, forget they were written by Heller and Jackson.'

I shook my head. 'He liked the attention more than I did. You know, Sammy Cahn once said that most songwriters look like dentists, but Max was an exception. He was handsome and talented, and even if his wife wasn't exactly Barbra Streisand, who cared? They made a good-looking couple. So while Patty and I got on with our lives, Max and Lorna kept the scribes busy and our songs benefited. I guess they got more exposure than they deserved.'

'For a while,' she said gently.

'Nothing is forever,' I admitted. 'Flower power came and went. Then there was heavy rock. All of a sudden it seemed that the songs Max and I were writing belonged to a bygone age. There was talk of a TV series, with Lorna and Rick Nelson, but Rick's career was in a tail-spin and it all came to nothing.'

'And then you and Max split up.'

'It was no one's fault,' I insisted, propping myself up in the bed. I shouldn't be talking so much, the nurse would scold me for tiring myself out. But what did it matter? 'Except perhaps it was my fault, for going down with pneumonia at the wrong time. Max and I had been asked to write a couple of numbers for a TV special. I got sick and finished up in hospital. The deadline was forty-eight hours away, so the television company asked Max to work with Chrissie Goldmark. They hit it off straight away. The songs they wrote were candyfloss, but by the time I'd recovered, they were talking to Scepter about producing a new album together. Not for Lorna, though.'

'Lorna didn't take that well, did she?'

'Could you blame her? Chrissie fancied Max, and like all men, he was susceptible to flattery from a pretty girl.'

Alice leaned close again. I supposed it was a trick of hers, a ploy to use when talking to men. A habit, almost. 'Were Max and Chrissie lovers?'

'What do you think?' Playing for time again.

'Everyone I've spoken to believes the two of them had something going.'

'Maybe they did. So what? It doesn't make Max a murderer.'

'Lorna was an emotional woman.'

'Emotional woman? Tautology, Alice.'

She wouldn't be riled. 'Lorna was tempestuous. Her career was fading and she hated that. She must have realised her looks wouldn't last forever. She was smoking eighty a day, her whole life was burning up. Losing her husband to a second-rate wordsmith would have been the last straw. I bet she wanted revenge. Hell hath no fury, you know. Maybe she threatened him with divorce, bad publicity...'

'Max never stopped caring for her. Besides, he wasn't a violent man.' Suddenly I felt very tired. Reaching back into the past was draining the life from me.

'Anyone can snap,' Alice said softly.

How could I deny it? Clearing the phlegm from my throat, I said, 'Max didn't.'

'Your loyalty does you credit,' she said, as I closed my eyes. 'But how can you be sure?'

'You're torturing yourself,' I told Max. 'And for no reason.'

'I don't have an alibi, you know. I was hanging out here on

my own while Lorna was in the house on Long Island. We'd had a fight. No point in lying to you, it was over Chrissie.'

I checked my fingernails. 'She accused you of having an affair?'

'Yeah, the morning she died. It wasn't an accusation, just a statement of fact. I didn't try too hard to deny it. She asked if I wanted a divorce. If so, she was willing to agree. She didn't intend to spend the rest of her life with someone who had fallen out of love with her. I said I didn't want to rush things and she made a coarse remark and things kind of went downhill from there. You know how it is.'

'So you came back here, to your old bachelor pad.'

'Lucky I kept it on, huh? I haven't had the heart to spend time on Long Island ever since she tumbled down that staircase. Fact is, I could have gone back and killed her, made it look like an accident after she'd been drinking. Which she'd been doing too much. The house is quiet, no one would have seen me come and go. Who's to say I'm innocent?'

He leaned back and the kitchen stool wobbled dangerously beneath him. The sink was piled high with dirty dishes, there were coffee cups filled with day-old instant Yuban. Looking out on to the terrace, I could see rumpled beach towels and grubby squeezed-out tubes of Bain de Soleil.

Following my gaze, he said, 'I've not been in the mood for tidying.'

'It won't do, Max.'

'Said like a true Englishman. Sorry for falling short in the stiff-upper-lip department, but the truth is, I'm pretty pissed about all this. All of a sudden, nobody wants to know me. Not even the woman I'm supposed to have committed murder for.'

'You're right,' I said suddenly. 'If you had an alibi, the tongues would stop wagging. You could start your life over.'

'Pity I screwed up by not having Chrissie round that night.'

'Where was she?'

'Jiving at some nightclub. Not my scene. I suppose I was

already realising she was a bad habit, one I ought to break. I was supposed to be working on a song, but I had a couple of beers, then a couple more. Before I knew what was happening, I was fast asleep. And then the next morning came the cops, knocking on my door to break the news.'

'Aren't you forgetting something?'

'Like what?'

'Patty and I called round here that night,' I said calmly. 'It would have been about eight. She'd persuaded me to make an attempt to bury the hatchet.'

He stared at me. 'What are you talking about?'

'Patty thought you and I made a good team. She's always been fond of you.'

'No, she hasn't.'

'It's Lorna she didn't like.' I sighed. 'Trouble was, you and I argued. We'd both had a few beers. I took a swing at you and missed. Patty decided it was time for us to go. Not long after nine o'clock, she checked her watch. By then you weren't in a fit state to go anywhere, and anyway, according to what I've heard, the authorities are convinced Lorna was already dead.'

His face was stripped of expression. I guessed he was calculating pros and cons. That was Max: he always played the percentages.

'Are you serious about this?'

'Never more so.'

'We don't have to drag Patty into this.'

I noticed the *we*. Progress. 'Sure we do. After all this time, we need to make it look credible. People might think I was simply trying to save my old partner's good name if I was the only one giving him an alibi. Trust me, Patty and I have been tossing it around for a few days now. She agrees it's for the best.'

He rubbed his chin. 'I don't know, Steve.'

'Yes, you do. It's the only way. I'll put the word around that I've only just got wind that people are seriously pointing the finger at you. You and I may not be working together any more, but I'm keen to set the record straight.'

'But…'

'No buts. You want to spend the rest of your life like some pariah? Think about it.'

I could imagine his mind working, testing my proposition, checking it for flaws. Of course he would go along with it in the end. He had no choice, if Lorna was not to destroy his life, the way she'd almost destroyed mine.

Lorna, Lorna, Lorna. I can still smell the gin on her breath, the last time we were together. Still hear her striking the match to light yet another Lucky Strike from the crumpled pack. Still see her cupping her hands over the sudden flame. Still see her flicking ash all over the imitation Versailles rug. She was just waiting for me to call her a slut, but I said nothing, let her scorn wash over me like breakers on the shore. Even now I cringe at the memory of the coarse words, all the more shocking because they came from a scarlet mouth as cute as a bow-ribbon on a candy box.

'So how are you today?' asked Alice as she set up the tape recorder.

I made a slight movement with my shoulders. The doctor had talked to me that morning. There wasn't much time left.

'You're flying back home tonight?'

'Uh-huh.' She studied me. 'I just want to say thanks for all your help. It can't be easy for you, re-living the past when you aren't well.'

'Those were the best years of my life,' I said. 'It's no hardship to bring them back to mind. You know, I never had another top thirty hit after the spring of '67. Thank God for Muzak. The royalties never stopped dribbling in, enough to keep Patty and me fed and watered.'

'What happened to her career?'

'Same as happened to mine, I guess.' I sighed, spoke almost to myself. 'Doesn't matter, it's been a good marriage these past forty-odd years.'

'She's coming to see you again this afternoon?'

'Never fails. The arthritis gives her hell, but she fights through the pain.'

'Did you stay in touch with Max?'

'Not really. We bumped into each other now and then. Last time I saw him must have been in the early Seventies, just before he was killed in that plane crash.'

'You never wrote another song together after Lorna died?'

'No, things never seemed to gell. Our time had passed.'

'So why did you alibi him for Lorna's death?'

Her voice had never sounded so sharp before. I flinched under her laser stare. 'I told you before,' I said. 'He didn't kill her.'

'Maybe he didn't,' she said. 'Maybe someone else did.'

All of a sudden, I felt very cold. 'What do you mean?'

'I talked to Lorna's best friend. After all these years, she's broken her silence, as the saying goes.'

'And?' My voice was no more than a croak.

'Lorna confided in her. Max's affair pissed her off. So she decided to take revenge by bedding you. Dear, dependable, happily married Steve. It helped prove how irresistible she was.'

'Girls talking,' I said. 'It doesn't mean a thing.'

She bent over me again. 'Did she taunt you? Or threaten your security? Maybe it was that. Perhaps she said she would spill the beans. You couldn't risk having Patty find out the truth. Was that why you shoved her down the stairs?'

'No,' I whispered. 'No, no, no.'

Lorna, Lorna, Lorna. The contempt in her glazed eyes that last time, when I told her life wasn't like writing songs. You can't keep changing partners. Nicotine-stained fingers jabbed into my guts as she told me to get out. No one ever dumped her, she said, *no one*. And certainly not a two-bit rhymester like Steve Jackson.

I could have killed her right then. Oh God, how I wanted to.

Patty arrived an hour later. All the time I've been in this place, she's never missed a day. Her love for me has never skipped a beat. She's been so faithful.

When I'd finished telling her about my conversations with Alice and the doctor, she took my hand. Hers was knobbly, deformed by the disease in her joints. I closed my eyes, recalling the smoothness of her skin when she was twenty-one.

'So she has her scoop, something to help sell her book? Lorna Key wasn't killed by her husband but by her lover, Steve Jackson?'

'By the time she publishes, I'll be dead and buried. She's made sure of that by taking a good look at me and having a few words with the doctor. No need for her to worry. A corpse can't sue for libel.'

Patty squeezed my hand tighter. 'I won't let her do it. I won't let you do it.'

'Don't be silly.'

'It doesn't matter now. I may be losing you, but not for long. I still have those pills I told you about. You must tell her the truth.'

'Why me?'

'You're the one who always had a way with words.'

'Lorna deserved to die.'

'No, she didn't,' Patty said. 'I was just a jealous bitch who killed another woman because I was afraid she'd wreck our marriage.'

Funny, she'd never talked about it before. And I'd never asked, there was no need. I'd guessed her secret as soon as she came home that night, the stench of Lorna's Lucky Strikes clinging to her clothes, to her hair, to her skin. She'd never meant it to happen, I always told myself. Lorna was just killed by an unlucky strike.

'She didn't succeed, did she?'

She kissed me lightly on the cheek. 'No, darling. No one could ever tear us apart.'

So there it is, Alice. How wrong you were. This isn't a murder mystery at all. It's just like one of those trite old lyrics of mine, you see. A tear-jerker, a heartbreaker. A story about love.

Margaret Murphy

BIG END BLUES

The moment I clapped eyes on her I knew she was trouble. So what did I do? You guessed it – I took a few steps back, broke into a run, and did a flying leap into her arms. That's me all over: always hitching my cart to the wrong pony. Thing is, she's got style, has Norma. They say imitation's the sincerest form of flattery – well, with us it wasn't so much imitation as co-ordination. Fact is, we wanted to make an impact, and since Norma's eye for colour and texture is more refined than mine, I went along with her choice. I mean in *every* detail. Skirt, blouse, jacket, shoes – even those little extras fashion shops call accessories. If Norma bought it, so did I. We shuffled the colours around a bit – well you don't want to look ridiculous, do you? But in all essentials we were identical.

It was Norma came up with our showbiz name. We were in a shop. Hers was a black denim jacket, red silk skirt, white scooped-neck T-shirt, mine was red jacket, black skirt – the tops were the same, as I recall. She looked at us, a glory of patchwork side by side in the mirror, and said it straight off: 'The Harlequin Twins'. It was a joke of course. You had to see us to get it. I sometimes wonder what folk made of us, her a tall, willowy blonde and me a short, well-stacked brunette.

She has a good length of stride, does Norma – pretty impressive in stilettos. If you've ever worn them, you'll know what I mean. She glides, I wobble, but only a bit, and very fetchingly, so I'm told.

We do a double act – on and off stage – Country and Western

mostly, and when the mood takes her Norma can carry the Mississippi Delta mouth and mannerisms into her everyday chat, like she was born to it.

We were having a bad day. A grey December afternoon in the north of England is depressing enough, but our transport was well and truly knackered, and it looked like we'd have to cancel our gig because we didn't have the wherewithal to pay for repairs. A grey December afternoon in the north of England with no escape route – that's when a girl's thoughts turn to suicide.

'Big end's gone,' the mechanic said, slamming the bonnet and wiping his hands on a filthy towel.

Norma fluttered her eyelids and did that thing where she half-turns and looks over her shoulder. 'Why thank you, honey,' she said, twanging all over the place. 'All that dieting's been worth the while.' She slid her hands over her perfectly toned buttocks just to hammer home the point, but he wasn't having it. She was wearing the white denim skirt – thigh-length (just) – and the fringed nubuck jacket in red. Shoes to match the jacket and morals to match the skirt – at least that's the gist of what she was trying to put over to him. He just narrowed his eyes and carried on wiping his hands. Must've been a poof. It's worked before: she gets the job done on the promise she'll make it up to him after we've got the van back – well, she can't very well have him handling the goods with those grimy palms, can she? Of course, by the time he arrives at The Dog and Duck, all spruced up in his best jeans and trainers, we're halfway down the M6, twenty minutes from our next gig.

In this case we were set up for a theme pub in Birmingham. All the staff dress up as cowboys and cowgirls. Four slots over two nights. The pay's all right, if you can manage your money, but Norma's got a hunger for shopping and we wouldn't be the Harlequin Twins if I didn't keep up, now, would we? Besides, on the road, you've got other expenses, like food and drink, make-up, equipment, but Mike the mechanic wasn't playing, and it looked like our motor problem would be the big end of a beautiful partnership.

We decided to think about it.

When Norma needs to think, she walks. So we walked. Every few steps I had to run a bit just to keep up. We fetched up a couple of miles away, near the docks. Empty warehouses on one side of the road, a flattened plot on the other. Someone had put up a billboard: *Industrial land with outline planning permission.* Some hope.

Norma stopped at the bus shelter and wiped the seat with a paper tissue, parking her bum carefully on the edge of the narrow yellow strip of plastic. Which made me think.

'Plastic,' I said, sitting next to her.

'No.' Norma has a rule – kind of a code of honour – never upset your credit-card companies. Why? Because they pay for your clothes. We were already up to our limit on account of the Birmingham gig demanding a new outfit each. 'No plastic,' she said.

I shrugged. They'd've probably checked our credit-worthiness anyhow.

Just then, a big, wheezy old removals van pulled up at the kerb, throbbing with pent-up bass rhythms. A bloke got out – well, I say bloke, using the term loosely. He was more simian than *sapiens*. Bloody huge, fat and all, but enough muscle so you wouldn't be tempted to call him names. He opened the cab door and the music boomed out, loud enough to rattle your teeth loose. He jumped down with a wrench of some sort in his hand. Big wide thing it was, with handles both ends, like a plane propeller – a device with wings, to avoid embarrassing slippage – only for men.

Norma looked over at him and said, 'Hey love, you couldn't turn that shit down could you?' In her normal voice. Nothing offensive, just a polite request.

He growled – no, seriously – he really *growled*, like a dog, only bigger and meaner. And twice as dangerous. He started towards us with that bloody great wrench in his hand and I think, *there's nobody between us and the river*. This bloke could do whatever he wanted and we wouldn't be able to raise a minor quibble, never mind an objection.

We ran. God knows where we thought we were running *to*, but when someone as ugly as that looks at you like that, you don't think, you just run – anywhere, so long as it's *away*. He lobbed the wrench and I got it between the shoulder blades. I went down hard, about halfway across the road.

I'm winded and crying. I see this shadow over me like in some horror flick and I roll over, so at least I can see what's coming. He bends down and lifts me by the front of my jacket and I think, *I'm dead*. Then I hear Norma, like her voice is coming from far off, but it's clear.

'Pooky,' she says, 'Now don't you be a big old bear. You know we didn't mean no harm.' Where she got Pooky from, I don't know. She's always coming up with names like that – she thinks they sound authentic Southern USA.

The big bastard drops me, and I fall on my back, whooping, trying to get my breath. Norma's standing the other side of me, smiling, swinging that shiny wrench back and forth between her legs. Her image doubles, quadruples, on and on, like a thousand tiny images in a glitter-ball and I think, *Oh, God no – Norma don't...*

She's paying the mechanic in cash. She doesn't waste a smile on him this time, just completes the transaction and leaves. I'm driving. The van's never sounded so good. We motor for a while with the radio turned down low.

'All right?' she asks.

I'm not, but I nod anyway, gripping the wheel tight to stop my hands shaking.

She sorted everything. Got him off the road, over to his lorry. I helped her drag him on a piece of tarp we found in the back.

It was empty aside from that one piece of ratty tarp. I said a prayer he had finished for the day, that someone wasn't waiting on a doorstep, checking the time, anxious for the removals man to arrive. We draped him over the engine and closed the bonnet over him. He looked like one of those joke dummies you some-times see halfway up a wall – Santa with a sackful of goodies, that kind of thing.

'It won't fool anyone, you know,' I say.

'Correction,' she says. 'It won't fool anyone *for long.*' Just long enough for us to get away, was the implication. I suppose she thinks I'm being ungrateful. 'In the meantime...' She digs into her handbag and fans a handful of cash. 'Enough to be going on with.'

I nibble my lip and she sighs. 'Okay, honey, one more time,' she says. She doesn't often turn on the Southern charm for me. My stomach lurches – because when she does, it means trouble. 'But this is the *very* last time.' She checks off the points on her fingers. 'Nobody saw us. We left no fingerprints. Not one bitsy clue. And it's not like he knew us. Who's going to suspect two sweet little ladies like you'n'me?' She bats her eyelashes and looks at me all innocent.

Nervous. She's definitely making me nervous, but I've got to admit she'd been thorough. Insisted on walking back into the city centre, rather than get a taxi, despite my bad back. She wore a disguise, so when she tried the PIN numbers he had considerately left along with his credit cards in his wallet, she was unrecognisable. I wouldn't have known her – her own *mother* wouldn't have known her in that get-up. Dark glasses, I would have expected, but she also wore a woolly hat – not a strand of hair showing – she even bought some cotton wool balls to stuff in her mouth and fatten her cheeks. I was impressed. Bear in mind Norma is vain: she doesn't make herself look plain without a damn good reason.

'They take pictures at cash-tills these days you know,' she told me. Proud of herself.

I'm proud of her, too. Me – I'd've walked in to the nearest cop shop and made a tearful confession. Ruined the rest of my life. Not Norma. Still I *am* nervous – kind of in awe of her.

'Pull over.'

I do as I'm told. A quick glance around and then she drops Pooky's wallet down a drain at the side of the road.

'Untraceable, see? And that's the end of it.'

I want to believe her, honest I do. But she's got that look on her, like the day she gave us our stage name, and I know that this is only the start. For Norma and Denise read *Thelma and Louise*. It's only a matter of time.

Stuart Pawson

FLOWER POWER

'This is one for the maggot man.'

I glanced sideways at the superintendent. 'Entomologist,' I said.

'That's right. You need him. Time of death.'

The body looked part of the landscape, camouflaged by the leaf mould that had been heaped over it. The head was visible, a mop of dirty brown hair, but you could have seen it a thousand times and not realised what it was. Only the legs, as bleached as a pirate's bones on the seabed, gave away the park's deadly secret.

We were squatting on our heels, watching the pathologist from the General making his preliminary examination, deep in our own thoughts. I'd skipped lunch to talk to a councillor about crime in the new shopping mall, and now it looked as if my evening meal would have to be snatched at some late hour, if at all. I'd call in Tesco's for some cornflakes and bananas on the way back to the station. That's all you need to sustain healthy life.

Meanwhile, there was the problem of the body. She was female; I was fairly certain of that but not totally sure. The lower legs were exposed where the foxes had scratched away the covering of leaves, which suggested a skirt, but their shape was indeterminate, thanks again to the attentions of the animals and the maggots. It's not in the textbooks, but men and women have differently shaped legs. I've made an informal study of the subject.

There weren't many flies, thank God, but plenty of maggots and pupae, which indicated that she'd been there quite a while. A few weeks, I guessed. The experts would give us a more accurate time, and if we identified her we'd probably pin it down to the very day.

The pathologist straightened up, grimacing with pain and rubbing his back. We did the same, rising expectantly to receive his conclusions. He indicated to the photographer where he would like some extra pictures taking and stepped over the cordon of blue and white tape towards us. Harsh experience taught me not to leap in with questions about time of death, cause of death and who she was. He knew what we needed, and he'd tell us what he could in his own good time.

The super had no such inhibitions. 'So how long has she been there, Professor?' he asked.

Professor Sulaiman glanced at me as he peeled off the latex gloves with practised deliberation and exchanged his reading spectacles for general purpose ones. He took a huge white handkerchief from a pocket and wiped his eyes before carefully refolding and replacing it. 'White female,' he stated. 'Cause of death unknown. Infestations around head and thighs indicate those areas to be the locus of injury. Lesser infestations on lower legs. Death probably occurred sometime in the spring and that's as far as I'm going.' He looked at me and said: 'I'd get Jake Westland in on this one, Charlie. He'll be in his element.'

'Full PM in the morning?' I asked.

He inflated his cheeks and let the breath out in one big puff. 'Yes, I think so. She's waited this long, so another few hours won't hurt the poor lass. And it will give you time to check your missing persons list. Will you be coming to watch, Charlie?'

I shook my head. 'No thanks, I'll delegate that little task. Unless...' I glanced at the boss, '... unless Superintendent Wood wants to be there.'

The super coughed and pulled back his shoulders. 'No,' he said. 'Not in the morning. Accountability meetings. I'll leave the details to you, Charlie, as long as you keep me informed. Didn't you ought to be arranging for the entomologist?'

'I'll do it now,' I said, turning to leave. 'Thanks for coming, Prof, and I'll speak to you tomorrow.'

A jogger had found the body, fifty yards into the woods that surround Heckley Park. He'd left the path, he said, to 'see if the orchids were out,' and was rewarded with a different harvest. Once upon a time it was men walking dogs who found all the bodies, nowadays it's just as likely to be a jogger. I walked to the road where our cars were parked, following the taped path we'd laid out. Vans belonging to the photographer and the SOCOs had joined the queue, and a patrol car with its light flashing warned passing motorists of the obstruction we were causing. Dave Sparkington, my DC, was standing on the foot-path, talking to two uniformed PCs from the panda and the SOCOs.

'Anything to report, Boss?' Dave asked as I approached them.

'No, nothing that you couldn't have guessed. Lots of wildlife, though. Did you contact Dr Westland?'

'Mmm, 'bout an hour ago. Should be here in thirty minutes or so if he drives like a lunatic.'

'That should impress Mr Wood,' I said. 'He's just told me to ring him. York to Heckley in half an hour is going some.'

'Dozy old buffer,' Dave stated.

'Now now, Dave,' I admonished. 'Not in front of the civilian staff.'

'Who's Dr Westland?' one of the SOCOs asked.

'King bee in the Entomology Department at York University,' I told him, 'and I'd like you to work in conjunction with him when he arrives. He should be able to give us a time of death from the way the various insects and maggots have inhabited the body.'

One of the PCs made a groaning noise. 'Aw, that's put me right off my tea,' he complained.

'Well it hasn't me,' I replied. 'Who's going to volunteer to fetch some sandwiches?'

Overnight we had four burglaries, one stolen car, a mugging, a domestic disturbance and a pub fight. Early summer is a quiet time. The mugger had struck before and three of the burglaries bore the trademark of a local junkie who just happened to have finished twelve-months youth custody the previous week. He was skinny enough to crawl through those little windows that people leave ajar for a bit of ventilation. Thinking about it, I've never met a fat burglar.

I read the reports, delegated someone to find him and cursed Dave for not ringing me. He was at the post mortem and supposed to keep me informed of anything he learned. At just after eleven I was on the phone explaining to the super why our monthly figures were late when Dave walked into the office, ushering Jake Westland in first.

The doctor is middle-aged and matinée-idol handsome. Black hair fashionably cut, all-year suntan and immaculate suit. Unfortunately he's only about five foot two, and the overall effect is of a ventriloquist's dummy. He compensates by driving an Alfa Romeo, and when it comes to creepy-crawlies he certainly knows his onion fly.

'Hello, Jake,' I said, extending a hand. 'Nice to see you again.' I tried not to crush his fingers, delicate as the Asian girl's who serves me at the corner shop, and asked him if he'd like a coffee. 'My trusty manservant was supposed to keep me informed,' I went on, nodding towards Dave, 'but he let me down again. Have you had an interesting morning?'

'I thought the doctor better tell you himself, Charlie,' Dave interrupted. 'All is not what it seems.'

'Very interesting, Charlie,' Jake replied. 'And working in conjunction with Professor Sulaiman allowed us to draw certain conclusions that may not have been so obvious had we worked in isolation.'

'That's what I like,' I told him. 'Conclusions.'

Flies, bluebottles and greenbottles, plus more midges, gnats and assorted flying creatures than you can shake an aerosol at, lay their eggs on dead bodies. Cats, horses, fish, human beings, rich or poor; it's all the same to them. They carry their egalitarianism to extremes. They are attracted by the smell of putrefying flesh, seek out a moist orifice in it and lay a few hundred eggs. The eggs hatch into maggots which gorge themselves on the decaying meat until they pupate, and the pupae eventually develop into new flies, or whatever.

The clever thing is, they have an arrangement. Every different species does it at a different time and at a different speed. Give Dr Jake a nice juicy corpse with an infestation of maggots and he can tell you when the very first ones arrived on it, which can often indicate time of death to within a couple of days.

'Our old friend *Calliphora vomitoria* was notably absent,' he began. 'This year it was on the wing from the middle of April, possibly a little later in sunny Heckley. That suggests that the body had ceased to hold any attraction for them by then. On the other hand, there were plenty of Scatopse notata larvae, plus pupae and puparia, which indicates...'

I held up a hand to silence him. 'Jake,' I began, 'for the benefit of Dave could you tell it in layman's language, please.'

'Right. Sorry. I have to say, it's a most interesting case, and one that I can't be too certain about until I spend some time examining my samples. However, preliminary indications are that there are few signs of blowfly infestation. As you probably know, shortly after death a body starts to lose its more volatile components...'

'It smells,' I interjected.

'If you insist,' Jake responded. 'And these volatile elements attract various insects. Blowfly are among the first to arrive, but after a couple of weeks the body, um, smell, changes and they are not attracted any more.' He smiled before adding, 'Presumably it becomes distasteful to them.'

Dave said, 'So she'd been there for a least a fortnight before the middle of April.'

'Mm, yes, it's looking that way,' the doctor replied.

There were four thin files on my desk. I reached for them, selected the most slender and extracted the only sheet of paper it contained. 'Jennifer Mary Hooley,' I read out loud and slid the page towards Dave. 'Aged thirty seven, lived on the Sylvan Fields estate, vanished without trace on April the third, the day after Mothers' Day.'

'Well,' he said, 'she'd had plenty of dental work done. Shouldn't be too hard to prove if it's her.'

'And what did Professor Sulaiman have to say?' I asked.

'Ah. This is where it gets interesting. Cause of death, laceration of the brain. She had severe head injuries, plus both femurs fractured and a broken pelvis.'

'That sounds like…' I began.

'A hit-and-run,' Dave said.

'Except,' the doctor added, 'he didn't run. Not at first. He stopped and dragged her body into the bushes, where he hoped it wouldn't be found for a while. Professor Sulaiman found evidence of dried pine needles in her nasal passages and trachea. It looks, Charlie, as if she were still alive when he left her.'

We had task-force officers doing a fingertip search of the area between the road and the spot where Jennifer Hooley's body was discovered. They found a handbag, complete with her railcard with photo and signature, about ten yards in from the road, buried in needles under a yew tree. It was the only evergreen in the wood – sometimes we get lucky. Jake Westland went back and found some of his beloved puparia under the tree and concluded that the body had been moved further into the wood after about two weeks. When we told the task-force boys it was a hit-and-run, they scoured the edge of the road and found shards of glass and plastic from what might have been an indicator lens. Things were coming together.

'Barry Keiron Hill,' Jeff Caton, one of my sergeants, stated as he entered my office the following morning with a smile as wide as the Horseshoe Falls.

'Never heard of him,' I replied, lowering the copy of *An Investigation into the Causal Links between Single Parenthood and/or Peer Pressure and Juvenile Offending* that I was pretending to read. 'Is he one of ours or one of theirs?'

He passed a sheet of paper to me, saying, 'Form for benefit fraud, stealing lead, running a scrap-metal business without proper records, and receiving. Oh, and a little matter of ABH – he likes to slap his wife around.'

'Charming,' I said, 'but is he one of ours or one of theirs?'

'Mr Hill,' he continued, 'actually telephoned us in the not-too-distant past, to report his car stolen. And blow me down if a few minutes later it wasn't reported on fire at the far side of Heckley Park.'

'They run a park-and-burn scheme in the Sylvan Fields estate,' I explained.

'And guess when this was,' he invited.

'Surprise me.'

'April the fourth, at one o'clock in the morning. That's the same night as Mrs Hooley died.'

I dropped my copy of *An Investigation into the Causal Links between Single Parenthood and/or Peer Pressure and Juvenile Offending* into the bin and slid my chair round to face Jeff. 'Sit down,' I said, 'and tell me all about it.'

We'd done our homework. Jennifer Hooley had been divorced for a year and lived in a rented house on the slightly more reputable side of the Sylvan Fields estate. Barry Kieron Hill lived just off the estate, in a stone cottage backing on to the

51

moors and more suited to keeping pigs in. It was surrounded by a patch of land littered with broken-down vehicles, rotting wooden huts and decaying caravans that he somehow earned enough money from to enhance his lifestyle beyond that allowed by the benefits he drew.

Mrs Hooley had worked as normal on the day she died, at an insurance office in Halifax. She was quiet and industrious – 'kept herself to herself' her colleagues told us, as if we couldn't have guessed. Once a week she had a special-treat night out, and the third had been such a night. She planned to eat in Debenham's restaurant after work and then go to the cinema, to see *Titanic* for the second time.

Her husband had been a womaniser and they suspected he was violent towards her. She'd finally left him, although it meant swapping her four-bedroom detached for an ex-council house on the Sylvan Fields. She'd been putting her life back together, learning to enjoy herself, when this happened. I paid a silent salute to her courage and promised her we'd do our best to give her justice.

We had a word with the husband but he'd been in Basingstoke at the time of her death, erecting scaffolding around a new superstore. He appeared cut-up when we told him about Jennifer, admitted he'd been a sod to her, but no doubt the sullen-looking blonde sitting on his chair arm, stroking his neck, comforted him after we left.

'Nice house,' Dave remarked as he closed the gate.

'And matching Toyotas,' I added.

'Plus the obligatory Range Rover.'

'Mmm.'

'When are we going to hit Barry Hill?'

'When we've something to hit him with.'

'He sounds a hard case. I can't see him breaking down and admitting it.'

'So you're sure he did it.'

'No doubt about it. Their paths crossed, right on the spot.'

We'd followed Barry Hill a couple of times and he appeared to be a creature of habit. He drove to a pub called the Duke of Wellington, favoured by the local hard men, teenage prostitutes and dabblers in narcotics. It was a traditional nineteen-thirties drinking establishment, long overdue for the fake beams and children's room treatment. The name of the licensee over the door was Brian Kilby Hill. Sounded like his brother. If Mrs Hooley had caught the last express bus home, she'd have had to get off about a quarter of a mile away and walk the rest of the way, because it didn't go round the estate. Her route and Hill's would have crossed on the lane where she was found. Not conclusive, but pretty heavy. He could have dragged her into the bushes and then driven to the far side of the park, where he torched his car. This would have left him with about a mile walk home. Twenty minutes. He'd rung the police from home to report the theft of the car. It was, of course, possible that someone had stolen the car and hit Mrs Hooley with it, but unlikely. They'd have just kept going. Stopping to hide her body was pointless for them, but for Hill it would have been a damage limitation exercise, even if it meant a death sentence for her. Dave was sure that Hill was the driver, and I agreed with him.

Mrs Hooley had her fifteen minutes of fame thanks to the local weekly and East Pennine Radio. The nationals gave her a mention and bunches of flowers started appearing at the roadside. We received the usual crank calls from Heckley's clairvoyant and our regular nutcase, and reports of sightings of Mrs Hooley began to trickle in, including some for after she was supposed to be dead. We investigated them all, including the clairvoyant, along with the more sensible offerings, but the lady had no skeletons in her wardrobe and her movements were well documented. She'd just been in the wrong place at the wrong time.

I was eating an M & S coronation chicken sandwich and

concluding a telephone conversation with my least-favourite councillor when Mr Wood blustered into the office. I held up a sticky finger to silence him, saying into the now dead phone, 'As a matter of fact, Sir, I'm in conference with Mr Wood at the moment, talking about this very issue. Would you like a word with him?'

The super waved his hands and shook his head as if signalling a no-ball and hissed, 'No! I'm not in.'

'Right, Sir,' I said. 'I'll put that to him.' I replaced the handset and mumbled an impoliteness.

'Was that who I think it was?'

'Yep. Complaining about truants shoplifting in the mall.'

'We'll have to have a blitz,' he said, 'get him off our backs. The ACC's secretary's been on about the figures again. Are they ready yet?'

'Um, no.'

'Well get them done, Charlie. And I've just had half an hour on the phone with the chairman of Heckley Comprehensive's school governors…'

'Good for you, Boss,' I interrupted. 'I'm sure the grandkids will be most happy there.'

'Not about the bloody grandkids,' he proclaimed. 'About the kids they've already got. Or not got. He reckons they're our responsibility when they're off the premises.'

'Even in school hours?'

'According to him. And if they're thieving it's definitely in our court. Like I said, we'll have to have a blitz.'

I was in the loo washing coronation sauce off my fingers when Dave came in. 'Anything?' I asked.

'Yep,' he replied. 'It peed it down all night on the third and the piece of amber plastic we found matches the front nearside indicator of a Cavalier similar to Hill's.'

'So we've got the car, if not the man.'

'Looks like it. Pity it's been crushed. You find anything?'

'Don't ask. And don't take your coat off, I think Mr Hill is due a preliminary visit.'

We drove over in Dave's, agreeing that at this point in the enquiry we'd only talk about the theft of Hill's car. His little smallholding looked almost picturesque with the sun on it and the cow parsley growing through the scrap vehicles that littered the place. Closer inspection revealed the oil-stained grass, the piles of bald tyres and the stink of a cesspit that badly needed emptying. An alsation dog on a chain started barking and leaping about as soon as we arrived, so I walked on Dave's left side, away from it. The cottage was small, two-storey, with a stone-flagged roof. Dave rattled the doorknocker and swiped at a fly that was determined to make a meal of him. I wafted one away from my face, saying, 'These flippin' *Callifudgit vomitaria* get everywhere, don't they?' Dave grinned and knocked again, but harder.

Mrs Hill answered the door and we flashed our IDs at her like we'd seen Starsky and Hutch do years ago. OK, so I never saw Starsky and Hutch, but Dave watched it and I copied him. She stood there as Dave introduced us, wearing a shabby housecoat and a bewildered expression, blinking in the sunshine. She was a reed of a woman, nervous as a rabbit, with what could have been the remnants of a black eye discolouring her cheek. She'd brushed her straggly hair across in an attempt to hide it.

'We'd like a word with Mr Hill about the theft of his car,' Dave explained. 'May we come in?'

'He's just getting up,' she replied, defensively.

'That's OK, we'll wait,' he said, stepping forward. She moved to one side and I followed him into the gloom of the front room.

The interior was a surprise: three-piece suite in brown velour with gold piping; heavy brocade curtains; Welsh dresser filled with Royal Doulton; wall-to-wall Axminster. The room was faded and cluttered, but clean as a bone. More china was on the sideboard and Oprah Winfrey was on the telly in the corner. Mrs Hill had been empowering herself. She called to her husband, saying that two men who said they were police had come to see him.

'Do you remember anything about the night the car was stolen, Mrs Hill?' Dave asked. A few minutes alone with her were more than we'd dare hope for.

'No,' she replied.

'But you must remember him coming home without the car,' he insisted.

'I was asleep.'

'It was raining heavily. He'd be wet through.'

'I don't remember. He told me about it next morning.' She produced a packet of cigarettes from the pocket of her house-coat and lit one with a plastic lighter.

'Was he upset about losing the car?' I asked. 'Or agitated?'

She pulled nervously on the cigarette and sent a stream of blue smoke towards the ceiling. 'Not so's you'd notice,' she replied.

The man himself bustled into the room, determined to sort out whoever it was violating his space on Earth. He had a head like the business end of an eight-inch shell and was wearing a singlet to show off his tattoos, with Adidas jogging bottoms.

'Can't you go outside to do that?' he snapped at his wife as she took another draw on the cigarette. She stubbed it into an ashtray and left the room.

'We've come about your car,' Dave explained after we'd flashed our IDs again.

'What about it? It was found burnt out, that's all there is to it.'

'What time did you notice it was missing?'

'What difference does that make?'

'Answer the question, please, Mr Hill,' I said.

After a pause he said, 'About quarter to eleven.'

'You left the pub before closing time?'

'So what's unusual in that? Bernie, my mate, leaves about then cos he 'as to be up early for t' market, so I call it a day then, too.'

Unknown to Hill another piece had fallen into place. Mrs Hooley's bus should have dropped her off at about five to eleven. If he'd stayed in the pub until after closing time we'd have needed a reason for her to be a few minutes late.

'So what did you do when you realised your car was missing?'

'I went back inside, didn't I? And told our kid about it.'

'Your kid?'

'Our Brian, 'e's landlord of t' Duke.'

'And what did he suggest?'

'Noffing.'

'Not even calling the police?'

He looked sheepish. 'Well, you know 'ow it is. I'd 'ad a couple of pints, 'adn't I?'

I said, 'A couple of pints as in a couple or seven,' and was rewarded with a glare that could have stripped the lead off a church roof.

'You didn't report the theft until almost one o'clock the following morning,' Dave told him.

'No. Well, like I said. I'd 'ad a couple; thought I'd best sober up a bit in case the fuzz came to see me. Needn't 'ave boffered, as it 'appens.'

'Was the car taxed and insured, Mr Hill?' I asked.

He scratched under an armpit and looked uncomfortable before saying, 'Yeah, 'course it was.'

'Could we see the documents, please.'

'Um, no. I don't 'ave them. I sent the certificate off for a refund. No point in making a claim for an old banger like that, is there?' He looked at Dave then back at me before adding, 'They only do you for your no claims bonus, don't they?'

We left him and walked back to the car, me on Dave's right this time as we passed the dog. Halfway back to the station

Dave said, 'No insurance. They live outside the law, people like him.'

I remembered a line from a Dylan song: *To live outside the law you must be honest*. He was right. If we were all honest we wouldn't need laws. Or policemen. Or solicitors and judges and jails. But we're not, so we do. I wound the car window down so as to catch the sun on the side of my face. After a few minutes I said, 'He doesn't smoke.'

'A small saving grace,' Dave commented.

'Think about it,' I told him, winding the window back up.

He looked across at me and was silent for a while. Eventually he said, 'I don't smoke and you don't smoke. So if we wanted to torch this car…'

'We'd have to buy some matches.'

I went upstairs to report to Mr Wood and walked straight into the councillor and the chairman of the school governors. The two of them nearly came to fisticuffs, but Mr Wood held them apart while I dodged about with the spit bucket. After more heated words and raised voices we agreed to blitz the mall in the morning with every available officer.

I spent the rest of the afternoon contacting the troops. Just after five I made myself a coffee and was about to phone Dave on his mobile when he rang me. 'I think we've cracked it,' he said.

'Go on.'

'Fina station on the bypass. Two minutes off Hill's route. Woman there picked him out from the mugshots and remembers him coming in. She works a three-week shift rota and was on nights that week, but can't remember the exact day. She's seen him around and he occasionally buys petrol there, but this time he didn't. They have a policy of serving petrol customers first, and he got a bit stroppy about being kept waiting, but she can't remember what it was that he bought. Could have been cigs, a sandwich or chocolate, that sort of stuff.'

'Or matches?'

'Or matches.'

'I think we'd better have him in.'

'Me too.'

'It's settled then. So go home and have an early night, for once.'

'Cheers. Is it a seven o'clock call for him?'

'Um, no,' I replied. 'He appears to be a late riser, so nine should be plenty early enough.'

A healthy diet is a varied one, and I believe in healthy eating, so I had rogan josh that evening. The night before, I'd had chicken jalfrezi, and the night before that it was tikka masala. I watched a football match on television and a video of *The Bridges of Madison County*, with Clint Eastwood and Meryl Streep. Most of the time I thought about the two women in the case. Mrs Hooley had made the break from her husband, Mrs Hill couldn't. She hadn't the nerve, the strength, the determination or whatever it took to leave him. Or maybe she came from a culture where you didn't abandon your marriage, choose what. And Mrs Hooley was dead, of course. At a primitive level she'd lost her man's protection when she left him. I went to bed and slept dreamlessly. I rarely dream, thank God.

We arrested Hill on suspicion of causing death by dangerous driving. He came quietly, but insisted on a solicitor before he'd open his mouth. Two companies have offices in the Sylvan Fields estate: one in what was once the Community Centre and one over the boarded-up chemist's shop. Some might call it progress. They advertise their services in their windows, like Amsterdam prostitutes, and have a regular clientèle. We sat Hill in an interview room with a beaker of coffee and waited for his brief to arrive.

'Tell us about the night your car was stolen,' Dave began, an hour later, after all the formalities.

'I've told you once.'

59

'Remind us.'

His story hadn't changed. The car had gone when he came out of the pub. His pal had already left and he'd had the proverbial couple of pints, so he walked home.

'Straight home?' I asked.

'Yeah, Straight 'ome.' We had him repeat it three times, just so there was no confusion.

'Inspector,' his brief said. 'It's obvious you have no evidence to link my client with this unfortunate woman's death, so I suggest we bring this farce to an end.'

'No,' I said, shaking my head. 'He's lying. We think he knocked her down and dragged her body into the woods, where she died some time later.' I turned to Hill and said, 'You might not have realised it, but she was still alive when you dragged her into the wood.'

'I wasn't there.'

'I don't know how it happened,' I told him. 'That road is unlit and she was wearing dark clothing. Maybe she stumbled off the kerb, right in front of you. You had no chance of avoiding her. Let's face it, it could happen to any of us. You thought she was dead, so you pulled the body off the road, into the wood, and drove away, torching your car to make it look as if it had been stolen. You panicked, and nobody could do anything for her, could they? Is that what happened? You're the only person who knows the truth.'

'No, I wasn't there,' he insisted.

'I think you were.'

'Well you're wrong.'

I pushed my chair back from the table as Dave leaned forwards on to his elbows. 'We have evidence, Mr Hill,' he stated, 'that on the night in question you called in the Fina station on the bypass at about eleven fifteen. Could you explain why?'

Suddenly he looked confused. 'No,' he mumbled.

'No, you weren't there, or no, you can't explain it?'

'I, er, don't know.'

'Try to remember.'

He looked at his brief for inspiration but was rewarded with a blank stare.

'OK,' Dave said. 'Here's an easy one for you. Am I right in believing that you don't smoke?'

'Yeah,' he admitted. 'I don't.'

'We have a witness who recognised you and there are video cameras at the Fina station,' Dave went on. 'You bought either some matches or a lighter. Why would that be?'

'I didn't,' he insisted. 'It's a mistake.'

'Or maybe you wanted them to torch your car.'

'Inspector,' the brief interrupted. 'I'd like a few minutes to confer with my client, if you don't mind.'

I minded like hell, but couldn't do anything about it. I looked at Dave, who was doing the questioning, and he shrugged his shoulders. 'Interview halted at ten fifty-five for Mr Fraser to consult with his client,' I said and Dave stopped the tape.

'C'mon,' I said when we were out of the interview room. 'Let's get to Mrs Hill, if we can.' The plan had been that Maggie Madison would baby-sit Mrs Hill while we interviewed her husband, but before I could organise it the super had deployed Maggie to the mall with everybody else. There were two possibilities why his brief wanted a word with him. Preferred choice was that he'd suggest Hill accept my explanation, come clean and go for a light sentence. His brother would swear on the life of his children that Hill had spent all evening sipping a bitter lemon, and we'd only have his word about how the accident occurred. We'd decided not to mention moving the body – that was a little surprise we were saving for if we ever got to court. The second possibility would be bad news for us. We staggered out of the station into the sunshine and piled into Dave's car. Eleven minutes later we were bumping down the track that led to Hill's cottage.

'Mrs Hill,' I said as she opened the door after the third

knock, showing my ID and pushing past her into the gloom. 'May we have a word?' I sat down as if I owned the place, but Dave remained standing, near the door.

'What is it?' she asked in a nervous voice.

I didn't answer for a few moments, transfixed by the mobile phone balanced on the arm of the easy chair, where she'd placed it a few seconds earlier. 'The night your husband's car was stolen,' I said. 'We were wondering if you'd remembered anything else about that night, or the next day?'

She was wearing the same wrap-around housecoat and her hair was still pulled across her face, Jean Harlow style, hiding the bruising. Once, not too long ago, she'd been attractive, but years of bullying by her husband had reduced her to a cowering, washed-out shell of whatever she'd been before.

'Yes,' she whispered. 'There was something.'

'Go on,' I invited.

'I, er, when he, Barry, that is, when he went out, I, er, asked him to bring me some cigs back with him. And some matches. He gave me them next morning. Said he forgot to get them at the pub, so he called in that garage on the bypass. Bought me twenty Bensons and a box of matches. That's all.'

'That's all,' I repeated, pinning her with my eyes. 'That's all, is it, Mrs Hill? Your husband dragged a still-living woman into the woods to die, and you say "That's all!"'

'I told you what happened.'

'No!' I snapped, pointing at the phone. 'You told us what he just told you to tell us.'

'He bought me cigs and matches.'

'He's a liar and a bully, Mrs Hill. Look what he's done to you.'

'He bought me cigs and matches.'

'I don't believe you.'

'Well it's true.'

'C'mon, Charlie,' Dave said, stepping forward. 'We're too late. Leave her be.'

We drove back at a more sedate pace. I broke the silence as we came off the bypass. 'Stop by the park, please, Dave,' I said. He knew where I meant and parked at the spot where we'd congregated on a dismal afternoon that felt an age ago.

A distinct path now led from the roadside to where Jennifer Hooley's body had been found. Someone had erected a wooden cross under the nearest tree and two sprays of flowers – carnations and freesias – lay in front of it. I squatted on my heels and read the tickets on them. 'Sorry, Jenny,' I said, quietly. 'I blew it. I did my best, but it wasn't good enough.'

I heard the crunch of Dave's size elevens as he came up beside me. 'They got the place wrong,' he said.

'Yeah,' I agreed, 'but I don't suppose she'd mind.' I pulled the flowers from their wrapping paper, saying, 'I don't know why they always leave them in the cellophane.' I scrunched it into a ball and laid the sprays side by side under the cross.

'Look here,' I heard him say from a few yards away. I straightened up and looked over at him. He was standing at the place where Mrs Hooley's body had lain.

'What is it?'

'Come and look.'

'What have you found?'

'See for yourself.'

There were dozens of them, poking up through the leaf mould and dog's mercury that covered the woodland floor. Tiny spikes of colour catching the dappled light. 'The orchids,' I said. 'I never knew these were here. What did the jogger call them?'

'Early purples.'

'Right.'

We didn't speak again on the way back. Dave's parking place had gone so he double-parked behind my car. 'So what's it to be?' he asked as he switched off the engine. 'Do we send him straight home or keep him guessing for a few more hours?'

I shook my head, bereft of words or ideas.

'We did our best, Chas,' he said. 'Sometimes it just isn't good enough. We'll hear from him again, believe me.'

'And his wife,' I added.

'Yeah. And her.'

I unbuckled my seatbelt. 'Those flowers,' I said.

'The orchids?'

'Mmm. Seeing them there, somehow, it seemed to help. Does that make sense?'

'I know what you mean,' he replied. 'Like a memorial. They've been there years – hundreds, maybe – popping up every spring for a few weeks, and they'll be there for a lot longer.'

'Mmm, something like that.'

As we entered the nick, Fraser, Hill's solicitor, rose to his feet from one of the chairs in the public part of the front office and walked towards us. 'This is most inconsiderate, Inspector,' he began.

'Have you advised your client to make a full and frank confession, Mr Fraser?' I asked.

'No, of course not,' he declared. 'Just the opposite. It's clear for all to see that you don't have a shred of evidence against him and that there is no charge to answer.'

I turned to Dave. 'In that case,' I said, 'you'd better book him out.'

I left them and trudged up the stairs to the office, wondering how many truants the rest of the staff had arrested in the mall. If they were having a good day our figures might not look too bad, after all. I put the kettle on and decided to risk either a vindaloo or a Madras for supper, just for a change.

Cath Staincliffe

ROCK-A-BYE-BABY

They wouldn't suffer. That was the whole point, wasn't it? They'd never have to suffer again.

The last weeks had been hard. She'd felt the resolution growing, spent days wrestling with voices, ceaseless arguments that spiralled to the same place and back. Everywhere Mary looked, everything she saw or heard only reinforced the picture of a world gone mad, bad and dangerous to live in.

When she turned the television on, the news spilled rivers of refugees: babies wailing, mothers with faces stretched in anguish, men wiping their eyes. Or stories of children mowing down their classmates with guns, of pipe-bombs shattering lives on sunny, urban afternoons, of night-raids and collateral damage, paedophiles and drug wars. Unbearable. She fumbled with the remote control, cutting off the images. When the children wanted the telly on she went and bought video tapes, cartoons and cutesy movies which they could watch over and over again.

She had unplugged the radio. She hadn't bought a paper for weeks and avoided reading the front pages at the supermarket. Then she avoided the supermarket. She did a big shop and stacked up on frozen meals, cans and dried food. When things ran out she used the corner shop, until – she shuddered at the memory and cast around in panic for thoughts to replace it.

The room looked beautiful: crisp, white linen, soft blue paint. Children peaceful on the bed. She watched the play of shadow leaves on the wall by the window. She had always loved this room, overlooking the garden with the tree just outside. Tree of Heaven, it was called. Graceful and airy with its fine, long leaves and arching branches. Like a filigree staircase reaching to the sky. That's where they were going. Heaven. Straight to Heaven.

They'd both been summer babies and she'd nursed them here in the dappled light from the tree. First Richard and then a year later Harry. She'd been fearful even then of harm befalling them. Finding herself so full of love she thought that it would break her. She guarded her babies fiercely, barely letting them out of her sight. She held her breath whenever her husband Jason lifted one of them, praying he would support the tiny head properly. Nothing had prepared her for the intensity of her feelings. The emotion she felt for Jason bore no comparison. The babies slept with her. He had the spare room. And then he moved out. It was hard to remember he had ever been there.

The seasons turned. The tree shed its leaves, danced in the wind, glittered with a dusting of frost, broke green again and grew. Jason sent money, she was careful with the budget.

Sandra next door had twins and sometimes they would get together and watch the babies for an hour, or walk to the playground. Sandra was very quiet and softly spoken. She never probed or pushed. It was easy to get away or put her off when Mary felt bad. She'd say Richard needed a nap or Harry had spiked a temperature or she'd ignore the knocking at the door and Sandra would leave her be. When the panic got bad she would climb in bed with the children beside her and tell stories until her voice wore out and her fear fell away with exhaustion.

The Health Visitor, who insisted on calling, suggested they go along to a Mother and Toddlers group. She said the children would benefit from the social interaction. She wrote down a list with all the places and days and times. When the Health Visitor had gone Mary chucked it in the bin. Social interaction. She gave them plenty of that: games and rhymes and songs. She played with them all day long. They didn't need anyone else.

It was nearly teatime, she could tell from the pattern of the leaves. Soon the sun would stream full into the room on its path west. Her drink was waiting. Drinking chocolate. She'd given them ice-cream. A small amount smothered with chocolate Treat to disguise the bitter taste. She promised them seconds if they ate it all up. They had both cleaned the bowls though Harry had pulled a face at the first mouthful. She told him it was cold as snow and he had grinned and dug his spoon in again.

She didn't sleep much anymore but she would lie and rest with the babies. Lie in the middle so she could turn to face first one, then the other. Gazing at perfect skin, at the soft down on Harry's cheeks, seeing the way the light sweat dampened the curls that framed his face and the suckling movements of his mouth as he dreamed of feeding. Watching Richard's eyes slide beneath the translucent skin of his eyelids, the tiny pulse beating in his neck and the spray of freckles on his nose, the occasional shuddering sigh as he shifted in his sleep, as if he had reached some great conclusion. She would move close and smell their baby breath, fresh like rain.

Sandra had asked her if she'd put the boys' names down for nursery. It made her feel sick. Richard should be starting next year, they took them at three and a half now. So young. Too young. She couldn't imagine taking Richard and leaving him, turning and walking away with Harry. A lamb to the slaughter. Who would love and protect him there?

She drank some of the chocolate. Fear bit at her neck as she recalled yesterday's letter. Eyes had scurried over print, words blurring. There'd been no warning on the envelope. One line stripped her nerves bare: 'to discuss custody and access arrangements.' She ripped the paper into tiny pieces, as small as possible, and put them in the bin. In the maw of the night she had risen and fished them out, put them in a pyrex dish and burnt them until only curls of ash remained. She scattered these on the soil round the tree.

Her thoughts veered away and collided with the corner shop. That last visit. She was lifting Harry out of the double buggy – she would never leave them outside alone – when a woman burst out of the shop dragging a small boy. The woman cursed at the child who was sobbing, his face a mess of snot and pain. Her voice was etched with hate. She swung out her hand and the boy ducked, which only served to enrage the woman more. She swore at him and punched him in the chest and slapped his head. He howled. The howling was in Mary's heart, too. A tidal wave of hurt and outrage rose, threatening to drown her. The woman slung a glance at Mary, her eyes burning and naked like a hunted animal's, her chin tilted up in defence or defiance. Mary cast her eyes down, busied herself with Richard's straps, her heart beating hard. She wanted to get them inside quickly, away from the ugliness. The woman dug her fingers into the boy's shoulder. Mary knew that grip. The slaps, the punches, the words that burnt like acid. Thank God, she said the familiar prayer, thank God she died before I had my boys.

In the shop she bought milk and bread, tried to push the images away, the grief of the little boy's face, the woman's challenging glance. She tried not to hear the shrill, cornered fury of the woman. She knew the pressure of that anger but she would never, never let it loose on her babies. It was safe, swallowed deep, deep down in her bones. Buried beneath the bricks of her mother's rage. Richard clung to her skirts, she held Harry on one hip. Something alerted the woman in the shop to her mood. 'You all right, love? You not been in much?' The kind words disarmed her. Tears sprang painfully in her eyes, choked at her throat. She nodded, blinking hard, hurried to pay and leave. She never let the children see her cry. She had learnt to weep silently, without motion, letting her tears slide onto the pillow as she gazed on perfection and wondered how much bigger love could grow.

She finished the chocolate drink and climbed into bed between her children. Their skin was cool now. She pulled the white covers close and nestled down until her face was level with theirs, a heavy head cradled on each of her shoulders, their bodies still small enough to fit within the curve of her arms. The sun poured in through the window. A breeze stirred the tree. The shadows tremored. She kissed Harry's head, where the curls met his temple, kissed Richard on the tiny bridge of his nose. My angels. She watched the leaves tremble. She closed her eyes and saw the honey glow of the sunlight. She began to climb the branches, up and round. Stretched out her hands, took their small ones in hers. No more tears. Safe now. Dancing in the tree tops. Full with love. Swaying up the steps to Heaven.

John Baker

AN OLD FASHIONED POISONING

Isabella went to the storage cupboard in which Miss Bristow's materials were kept. She cut from a roll of white linen a piece two yards long. In the kitchen Lucy and Louiscarl were laughing. Lucy had a black eye from their last drinking bout the night before. Tonight they were drinking cider and Louiscarl's laugh was as mad as Lucy's. Isabella folded the linen and put it in a bag with a glass jar half filled with vinegar. She understood the shortness of Louiscarl's lifeline. She knew why they had met and the part she had to play in his destiny. In the last few days she had returned time and time again to Grandmother Agnus's stories of death, and her own knowledge of effective poisons. She left the mill by the rear entrance to save herself the sight of her mother and her lover.

It was late evening and the dew had begun falling. Isabella felt the cold and wet on her feet. The moon was almost full but misted over, and a handful of stars had the entire night sky to themselves. Isabella walked away from the cliff, across Todd's meadow, through the copse and over the stream to the place where the ash were growing. There she inspected the leaves and smaller branches of the young trees for several minutes. But she did not find what she was looking for and eventually picked up her bag and continued walking.

A bush of lilac on the edge of the stream was more fruitful. She spread the linen on the grass under the lilac and set about shaking the shrub, occasionally stopping to inspect the debris that fell from leaves and branches.

She selected the bright, iridescent, golden green or bluish coloured bugs, all of them between a half and one inch in length and popped them into the glass of vinegar. Locally they were known as blister beetles, but Grandmother Agnus called them Spanish flies. At this time in the evening they were easy to collect, being dull and bedewed and unaware of what was happening to them.

From the first bush Isabella collected seven of the bugs, but before returning home she visited several other bushes along the stream. Her glass was full.

At the mill Louiscarl and Lucy were already in bed, cackling away together at some huge vision the cider had bestowed on them. Isabella took her dead blister beetles from the vinegar and strung them together with thread. She hung them over the chimney breast and stoked up the fire to dry them as quickly as possible.

When they were ready she put the beetles in a dry glass with a stopper and hid them away under her bed. It was the hour before dawn. The house was silent. She opened the door to Lucy's room and looked in at the couple on the bed. Alcohol hung in the air. They were both naked, lying across and over each other. Lucy slept with her mouth open, her arms thrown back on the pillow like a child. One of her teeth was missing, knocked out in the battle they called love. Louiscarl snored loudly. His face was a mask.

Isabella took over the cooking. Louiscarl did not complain about his portions. The Spanish fly, reduced to a fine powder by pestle and mortar, did not, at first seem to stay his appetite. He wolfed his food and returned to the sawpit. During the next days he became lustful and wanton. He cornered Isabella in the woodshed after breakfast and squeezed both her breasts, panting heavily. She pushed him away and he stood back from her, stroking his erect penis through his trousers. He came for her again, lifting her skirts and tugging at her drawers. She

71

stamped on his feet and escaped to the house.

Whenever he passed Lucy or Isabella he reached out to touch them, caressing a shoulder or stroking the line of the neck. He pinched their bottoms and sometimes made a grab for a handful of buttock. On the third day he took Lucy over the kitchen sink in mid-morning, twisting her arm up her back until her eyes watered, had her again in the sawpit after dinner and dragged her off to bed in the evening while it was still light.

During that night he left Lucy asleep in bed and came for Isabella by the back door. She did not fight him but nor did she satisfy him. In the morning his erection was still present and at breakfast his eyes were dark and brooding.

'We should all go to bed together,' he said.

Lucy laughed.

Isabella went quickly to her room and locked the door.

She doubled the dose. Louiscarl spewed his dinner into the bucket while milking the cow. His shit turned to liquid and ran down his legs. His urine came in drops and at each drop he let out a loud shriek of pain. He shook. His teeth chattered and his eyes watered. He dragged his body upstairs and dropped on the bed. Isabella took him a bucket and a cup of water.

Lucy sat with him. Next day Isabella prepared food but he refused to eat. He fasted three days and regained some strength. He walked to the sawpit and gazed into it abstractedly for some minutes. Then returned to the house and sat in the chair by the grate. In the early evening Isabella gave him a slice of toast with potted meat and Spanish fly. He turned blue and there was blood in his vomit.

Lucy took him to her bed. Isabella cleaned up the mess on the wooden floor. In the vomit the shining elytra which make up the wing cases of the fly reflected the fading light of the day.

'He can't pee,' said Lucy from the stairs. 'He wants to pee but he can't. We should get a doctor.'

'No need,' Isabella assured her. 'He'll come round.'

During the night his lips became hot and painful and a series of small blisters appeared around his mouth. By morning the blisters had coalesced to form a large sac filled with fluid. Louiscarl was deformed and dejected. He wanted to vomit but his stomach was empty. He needed to pee but was unable to squeeze out a single drop.

'He's getting worse,' said Lucy. 'We *should* get a doctor.'

Isabella was sure a doctor was unnecessary. 'He'll come round,' she said. 'I think the potted meat was off.'

Louiscarl was dying, but very slowly. After a few days fasting he made his way down to the chair by the grate. Isabella waited her chance and fed him more Spanish fly. He retired again to bed. He complained of pain in the region of his kidneys. He lost weight and the bones stuck out in his chest and shoulders. His eyes stared like great marbles in his head.

'I want to get in that sawpit,' he said at least once a day. 'I want to get well again, out in the sunshine. Back in the sawpit.'

On the eighth of October they heard of the death of Tennyson and Louiscarl dragged himself downstairs. He sent Isabella for a newspaper and she bought rat poison at the same time. The Spanish fly would work in time, but he had suffered enough.

'He died at Aldworth,' Louiscarl said, his head deep in the newspaper. 'His house, closely screened by plantations. And he's to be buried in Westminster Abbey on the twelfth.' He looked up from the newspaper. 'I want to be there. I want to be in London for the funeral.'

'You're not well enough,' said Lucy, shaking her head.

'We'll see,' said Isabella. 'Let's wait and see how you feel.'

'Listen,' said Louiscarl, his eyes fixed on the newsprint. '"With the splendour of the full moon falling upon him, his hand clasping his Shakespeare, and looking unearthly in the majestic beauty of his old age, he passed away on the night of the sixth of October."'

'Very nice,' said Lucy.

'Yes,' Isabella agreed. 'Very nice.'

Louiscarl smiled for the first time for weeks. 'He was reading *Cymbeline* when he died.'

Louiscarl did not attend Tennyson's funeral at Westminster Abbey. Isabella fed him the rat poison on the eleventh of October and the strychnine killed him within half an hour.

A few minutes after eating the stew he complained of stiffness about the neck and a look of terror came over him, as if he had a premonition of calamity. His head was jerked back and his arms and legs thrown forward. Lucy screamed. Louiscarl's chair overturned. Isabella leapt to her feet. Louiscarl was on the floor, his back arched. His weight resting only on his head and heels.

After a few moments he relaxed and Lucy bent to soothe his brow. The spasm returned immediately. While the women stood back and were quiet he relaxed, but at the slightest movement or when one or other of them touched him, he sprang back into the bow of his head and heels. The spasm and relaxation alternated rapidly for the next half hour. He had difficulty in swallowing, his eyes were wide open and fixed and his mouth drawn ugly aside.

When the symptoms passed he was dead. Lucy sank to the floor beside him in a faint. Isabella's face was wet with tears.

She sat on the edge of the bed, her hands gripping the counterpane. Lucy was moving around downstairs. Louiscarl's bookshelves lined one wall of Isabella's room and she cast her eye along the top row of books. The titles came into focus, into consciousness for the first time. Suddenly she could read them. *Confessions of an English Opium Eater, The Poetical Works of John Keats, The Rights of Woman, Childe Harold.*

Lucy's footsteps sounded on the stairs. Isabella felt a chill move up her spine but she did not move.

The Lady of the Lake, Oliver Twist, Middlemarch, Erewhon, Dr Jekyll and Mr Hyde.

The door opened and Lucy walked into the room. She carried the pestle and mortar. 'You done it,' she said.

Isabella looked away. *The Rubaiyat of Omar Khayyam, Huckleberry Finn, The Raven, Moby-Dick, Faust.* She looked back at her mother. 'I'm going to read all his books,' she said.

'He shouldn't have hit you,' Isabella told Lucy.

Lucy laughed. 'That's what they do,' she said. 'They all do it.'

'He didn't hit me,' said Isabella. 'He never laid a finger on me. He was gentle. Always gentle.'

'No,' said Lucy, laughing madly. 'They twist your arms and blacken your eyes. That's what they like best.'

They carried him out to the sawpit. He was buried there with the remains of the rat poison and the Spanish fly, with the pestle and mortar and a copy of *Cymbeline*. 'He'll appreciate that,' said Isabella. 'All he wanted was to get back in the sawpit.'

In Mousehole people assumed that Louiscarl had grown tired of the women and left. There was a rumour that the gypsy woman and her daughter had done away with him. But it was just gossip, for he was still there. He roamed through the house. He sat in the chair by the fire, reading his books. Late at night, when Isabella was ready for sleep, he came slowly up the stairs and got into bed beside her. And in the early morning when she woke, she could hear him outside in the sawpit, cutting his timber.

Chaz Brenchley

UP THE AIRY MOUNTAIN

Up the airy mountain,
Down the rushy glen,
We daren't go a-hunting,
For fear of little men.
> William Allingham, 'The Fairies'

The dead are heavier than they used to be, before they were dead. That's not what the scales say, but it's a fact none the less. Life is anti-gravity; the earth may suck, but we spit back at it and snicker, and walk just a little taller than we ought, step a little further, not float but – well, you get the picture. You live the picture, you should know. Every cell in your body resists that tug a fraction, and that's a lot of resistance.

The dead don't have the same privilege, it's all switched off. Meat, bone, body: heavy stuff. Even blood has weight to it, when the fizz has gone.

And when you're dying, when you're neither hale and whole nor wholly here, when your cells are slowly, slowly shutting down – that's when you start to acquire that extra weight, what can't be measured on the machinery but only on the minds and muscles of those who care for and about you, either or both. The dead are worse, the dead can overtopple a man with sheer mass, but anyone on that journey starts to acquire drag, momentum, matter, call it what you will.

We're all of us dying, of course, from the moment that we cease to grow; only that some of us go faster, and too soon.

As Glen, as he lay upon his bed and turned his head to find me and even his gaze weighed more than it used to, even his lightest thoughts had substance now.

Life is anti-gravity, and so am I; I hated to see him grave, portentous, sinking.

'Who is that,' he said in his horsehair voice, a fibrous scratching of it string on string, the only noise he had remaining to him, 'who's there?'

Who is that one who always waits beside you? Except, be fair, I thought, it might have been any one of us.

'Glenda honey,' *blood brother, lazy angel, open your eyes,* 'it's me.'

'Daniel?'

'Yes, lover,' and the third time that he'd asked today and it was hard to hold my patience except that I would, of course I would, what in God's name was I here for unless to do the hard things?

'Daniel. I want you to do me a favour. Big one...'

What, more than my being here and doing this? I'd fetched him bedpans until he couldn't manage, until so little movement hurt and he hadn't the control in any case. He was in big man's nappies now, and I changed them for him on my turn of duty. And I held buckets that he could gout blood into when that was needful, when he haemorrhaged inside and it had to go somewhere and generally came up; and I endured the hellwatch of his dead eyes, which was worse, and bathed them hourly in glycerine and water. And still turned up on time, on schedule, day or night. I caught a lot of night-time watches, often on my own. And came because he was my friend, or had been, and one of us at least had not forgotten. I couldn't imagine any favour greater than that.

'Daniel?' Seemed he hadn't forgotten either, or not right this minute. Sometimes he had never known me, ever; sometimes we were still bed-bunnies in his head, flashing rumps across a disco floor. Occasionally, rarely, we could be simply what we were in my head: old friends together, patient and nurse, one who claimed and one who paid the debts of long-gone loving. Those times he recognised my voice and called me by my given name, as now.

'Right here.' Sitting on the high bed's edge and laying my fingers lightly on his own, as much contact with the world as he could bear.

'Listen.'

'I'm listening.' Every word cost him pain and effort, precious coin; neither one of us would waste them.

'You remember that dog, where we put it, where we dug it under?'

'Christ, Glenda–!' As often as not he couldn't remember me, and yet he clung to the death of a dog, a nameless stray...

Well, yes. If I was Daniel, he was still or again my Glen, and he'd always held that animal in mind. Why else would I have remembered it myself?

'Yes, love, I remember the dog, and I know where it's buried. What of it?'

'Dig it up, Daniel.'

'What? What for?' Old dead bones that he'd broken himself, knocked all out of kilter even before the worms and the weight of soil and rock got to them; what was he going to do, cast an augury?

'There's a body, a boy underneath.'

'Oh, Christ.' He hissed, as my hand tightened; pressure hurt. How much had this hurt him, how long? 'What is this, confession?'

'Absolution.'

Glen, man, don't be in such a hurry... But he was, he had to be, of course. His time grew shorter, every breath he took; every moment's struggle wore him down.

'All right, then. Who's the boy?'

'I can't remember. You find out, Daniel, give him back to his family, let them bury him for real...'

When we went, we went as a team, as we were nursing Glen: his fairy band reformed, all but silent under the weight of him when we were in the flat together and utterly silent now, crammed into Henry's 4 x 4, compressed with news.

Henry, Jody, Tim and Blake and me. Tosh had stayed behind, hospital duty, nothing could break that schedule; something of him had come in the car regardless. We carried his curiosity along with his crowbar and shovel, along with our memories of the boy he used to be. We were all of us bonded, beyond the abilities of time or change to part us.

Once we'd been young and foolish, young and rowdy, high on the delights of city life and our own sweet selves, the damage we could do. Once we'd been wild together, following Glen or trying to grab the lead from him and never quite achieving that but loving him regardless.

No longer. Now we were a team again despite him, because of him; we didn't have a captain.

If we'd been kids still, eighteen, twenty, we'd have been arguing as we drove, wrestling for that elusive leadership: every band of fairies needs its Oberon. Grown men, it seemed, could get along without.

I might have claimed the crown for a while, at least, for a little while. It had been me that Glen had turned to; it was me that knew the way. The others only knew the story. For a wonder, they hadn't been there when the dog died. Seeking a little transitory independence, perhaps, looking for a new order, or simply sipping city lights on their own to find out how they tasted apart from Glen's direction, my own more subtle influence. Whatever. They'd been off without us, and they didn't know what I knew.

'Where now?' Henry demanded, slowing as the headlights

showed him how the road divided, left and right.

'Up,' I said unhesitatingly. 'Just keep going up. I'll shout, when we're near.'

The road climbed the hill, a high moor north and west of the city. It had been a night like this, I thought, when the dog had died: cold and clear, stars and a bright moon, the planet spinning us relentlessly toward a terrible uncertainty. Only difference was, in those days I'd seen hope and wonder in that spinning, in every dawn and sunset. Very heaven, I'd thought the world to be; and myself lieutenant to a power, a principality who held the keys to every pearly gate. I was young, I was a believer: music, dance, drugs, sex, whatever came along I gave it credence, I had faith. I believed in myself, my body, every way it made me feel. Money was votive, it allowed the opportunity to feel more, or feel differently. Even my hangovers I cherished for their immediacy, their potent size.

Outside my skin I was less certain, perhaps, but I believed in the band, our brotherhood, its tangibility against an insubstantial world. Above and beyond them all, I believed in Glen. He was that little bit older, that great gulf wiser: wherever we went he'd been there before us and knew his way about, whatever we came up against he could find a route through or over or around.

Even now, I supposed, he was leading the way, going first. Checking out the other side. If death was the last taboo, he meant to break it. He'd said that, more than once, before he got too sick to be clever.

Actually, I thought, he'd broken it already, long ago. Swift and hard and meaning every moment, and I'd watched him do it, I'd been sitting right beside him as he did. For a while, later, I'd thought it was for my benefit, a baptism of blood, a lesson given and learned. Now I wasn't sure.

*

The night cold and clear, moon and stars overhead but other lights were brighter, nearer, the whole of the city laid out before us like a playground, like a school; just the two of us in Glen's big car, and I felt special, selected, exhilarated. This didn't happen often, and it was treasure to me. Whatever he had in mind, I was up for it.

I thought...

We drove down the hill from his place towards the city centre, going slow; his eyes flickered constantly off to the side, to where long terraces and alleys fell away towards the river. Suddenly he knocked the indicator, spun the wheel, dived across the flow of traffic. Horns blared behind us, but he showed no sign of caring.

We were in one of the alleys: high walls of brick on either side, wooden gates and redundant coal-hatches, black bin-bags spilling garbage under our wheels. Ahead of us, eyes shone briefly pale in the headlights. A stray dog, young and hungry, all legs and ribs as it scavenged in the gutters; good street-sense it showed, cringing back against a wall to let us pass.

Glen steered straight for it.

It turned and trotted into its own long shadow, staring back over its shoulder; its eyes gleamed again, bright and empty. For a moment it reminded me of us, any one of us, skinny and scared and bathed in light, running into the dark.

It was running for real now, senselessly down the middle of the alley, forgetting what wisdom it had learned. Glen grinned, or showed his teeth at least as he stamped on the accelerator.

And me, I just sat and said nothing, did less, didn't even breathe. I was out there with the dog, sharing its thoughtless terror; I was in here with Glen – my friend, my mentor, my idol – and not sure if I were sharing anything with him. Either way I was trapped, inconsequential, the entire victim.

We thought we were the children of the night; looking back, I think perhaps we were all of us victims, all the time.

*

'There. By that outcrop, there's a place you can pull off to park...'

Probably we weren't meant to park there, it was an over-taking spot where the single-track lane widened suddenly and briefly between its enclosing dry-stone walls; but there was no traffic this time of night, we'd met nothing coming down as we went up. And no wardens, of course, no watching eyes. That was, that had always been the idea.

We climbed out slowly into the road and stood stamping and huffing, swinging our arms the way you're supposed to, the way you learned to do by reading it or seeing it in other, older men. The way we learned most of our adult habits: from books and magazines at first and then from men. It's a boy thing, unless it's just a fairy thing. Perhaps we were enchanted; God knows, we always felt that way.

Blake, Blake the builder reached back into the 4 x 4, dragged out a canvas bag of tools and passed them round. Pickaxe for Tim, crowbar and sledgehammer for Jody; for me it was three spades and carry-the-bag. Henry got nothing but a heavy torch; Henry had a banker's belly now, was furthest gone from lean and whipcord boy. Besides, it was Henry's car, he'd driven it, he'd done his share. We'd always been more socialist than democratic, dividing up the portions with a grand inequality. From each according to his ability: let him hold the light now, let him act as witness if we need one. Not objective, not neutral, never that – one for all and all for one, we few, we fairy few, immutable and indivisible and us – but he had the status we still lacked, he could speak for us if occasion demanded, and better he didn't have mud beneath his nails at the time. Real mud or figurative. It might not make a difference, but it might.

I led them up to the outcropping rock, to where a buttress thrust suddenly from earth.

'Here?' Henry asked, breathing heavily.

I shook my head. 'Not enough soil, it's bedrock six inches down. We tried it. Look, see that solus rock on the skyline there?'

They looked, saw, confirmed it with grunts and nods.

'Twenty paces, on a direct line from here,' and my hand slapped the buttress, 'to there. That's where we put the dog.'

'That's a bit – specific, isn't it?' Tim murmured at my back. 'A bit Treasure Island, X marks the spot in crutch-lengths, Long John Silver?' Tim the Crim, he was a lawyer yet, sharp to spot unlikely detail.

I shrugged. 'That's how Glen wanted it. He wanted to know, exactly; he said it was important. You couldn't just dump a body and forget it, he said. Even a dog's body mattered…'

I stopped, listening to myself on half a second's lag and shivering suddenly for better reasons than the night could offer me.

'He was setting you up, Dan. Just in case. Christ, he even told you so. Dogsbody, right?'

Well, at least he said that I mattered…

The dog died in silence, as it had run, pretty much as it had lived, I thought: lurking, sneaking, the opposite of presence. It was the car that made the noise, a thud that shook all the windows and rattled the doors; it was my mind that held it, that has held it ever since, one of those pivots a life can twist around.

Glen had been iconic, up till then. Suddenly he was something more, darker-stained and incomprehensible and human. We understand our idols all too easily, because they're invested with public virtues and public vices and nothing else. Only real people have private lives; Glen had just admitted me to his.

Though even then it was obvious that this was not habitual, he didn't kill stray dogs for a hobby. He stopped the car, as quietly as the dog had stopped; he got out and paused for a moment, looking at deductible damage – a bend in the bumper, a wet smear and a ripple on the dirty white bonnet – before he moved back up the alley to look at what was a fixed cost, no deposit and no return.

This was what I was there for, though I couldn't figure why. The sums wouldn't add up. Some kind of initiation, surely: maybe he put every boy through it, before they could melt seamlessly into his little band of brothers…

And swore them to silence after? Well, maybe. I didn't believe it, though. One of them surely would have said. And what was so significant about a dog's death, anyway? To us, who were not dogs – far from it, we were gorgeous, radiant, the height of delight – and dealt in worse fates daily? We knew all about death already, though he hadn't yet plunged among us in red braces, *greed is good*, as he would a few years down the line. The milieu we moved in, of course we knew. We danced on a deliberate edge, for the thrill of it; other boys had fallen off.

Still, I thought this was a message, expressly for me. I went to join Glen, where he stood above the mangled body; he said, 'There's a blanket in the boot. Want to fetch it?'

The boot wasn't locked. I found the blanket, ancient and moth-eaten, waiting for me; beneath it, I found a spade. None of this was normal, in Glen's car.

He made me do the messy work, down on my knees in the gutter, getting blood and muck on my dancing-clothes as I wrapped the dog in its ready shroud; he made me carry it back and stow it in the boot. I saw him smile faintly, as I wiped my hands on a corner of the blanket.

'Blood washes off, Daniel,' he murmured. 'Everything washes off in the end, and there's plenty of water in the world. Come on.'

He drove us out into the country, north and west; he parked on a high moor, found a landmark, paced a counted distance before he tossed me the spade and told me to start digging.

He didn't say much else, then or later, after he'd taken me back to his house and washed me thoroughly, teasingly, laughingly, working hard to win a laugh out of me; nor after he'd taken me to his bed, when we lay languid and weary and needing another wash. If any or all of this was a message, I thought it was missing me. If it was an exercise in bonding, bondage, I thought it was unnecessary. He should have known that I was bound already...

These days he didn't say much at all, and less that made sense. If this was an exercise in futility, I thought I might face a little grief from these old fairy friends of mine, here or in the car going home. If they let me get in the car to go home. They might leave me to walk if I'd dragged them up here on a fool's errand, in pursuit of fool's gold, buried treasure, buried bones.

Not my fault, but they'd blame me anyway, I thought. I was catching one or two looks already as we paced and counted, hefted hardware, faced the reality of chill air and frost-hard ground.

It wasn't that hard to dig, once you'd broken the crust of it; I remembered that from last time. And told them so, and caught a glare full-force from Henry. It was only the torchbulb glaring, I couldn't see his face, but it carried intent enough for anyone to read.

'Glen dreams,' he said. 'Hallucinates. What the fuck are we doing here, anyway?'

'Looking for a body.' *You brought us, you know...*

'What body? Anyone here missed a boy? It's just Glen, he's half mad with it, lesions in his brain...'

'Maybe so. He sounded clear to me,' and maybe it was my fault after all, maybe I did deserve all the grief I might yet receive, if I couldn't tell when the captain was seeing true and when he was simply babbling. 'Let's just dig, shall we? See where we get?'

Tim swung the pickaxe; Jody cracked the ground the way he used to crack doors, safes, whatever, with swift and judicious use of crowbar and sledge. I plied a shovel, as Blake did beside me.

Soon Jody abandoned the crow and grabbed the last of the spades. We built up a quick stack of spoil; I was relieved when Tim yelled out, I'd just been starting to wonder if I'd struck quite the right spot after all, because surely I hadn't buried the dog that deep.

'What?'

'Pick went through something. Not earth, it didn't feel right. Dig here. Henry, give us some light...'

We dug there in the circle of torchlight and scraped soil back off the rotten remnants of a blanket, with the rotten remnants of a dog beneath, snapped bones linked by slimy stringiness. Only the skull seemed whole, and only for a moment; it crumbled as Tim worked the pickaxe blade beneath.

I made some noise, I guess, some protest; he said, 'We're not archaeologists, Dan. Nor priests. This isn't what we're here for.'

No. And it was only a dog, in any case, and never mind that I'd seen it die and thought now that it might have died for this precisely, to be what people found if they should dig here.

Even so, 'Treat it gently,' I said, 'show some respect. We've got to put it back after, whatever else we find.'

'It's dead, Dan.'

'That's my point.' A sacrifice, a victim: we all knew how that felt. I felt understanding settle like the silence, all around me; we shifted that dog in spadeloads – Tim was right, we were not archaeologists – but did it as gently as we could manage, and laid the bones all together in a separate place. We wouldn't get them back in any order, but at least its ghost could find itself again.

Beneath where the dog had lain, we needed pick and crow once more, to work through hard-impacted earth. A forensics genius, I thought as I hacked uselessly with the spade's edge, an expert with light and time and tender loving care could say this had been stamped to such solidity. We had none of those advantages, but worked a little slower as it started to make sense. I felt happier, less happy, both at once. No trouble in the car, perhaps, but plenty after.

Even doubting Henry watched us closely now, slipping torchlight under every clod of earth we raised, looking for another gleam of bone.

And spotting it, first among us all, and crying out to warn us; we stepped back in a moment, rested on our tools, rubbed hot sweat from our faces and felt the cold touch of the night come back to claim us.

'There,' he said, pointing with the torch, close as a finger, 'see it?'

We saw it, just a streak of pale in the dark; and now I did want to play archaeologist, I wanted to get down and grub with my fingers in the dirt.

That was too much respect, we couldn't afford it. More cautious spadework then, the most care we could manage; in ten minutes we'd laid him bare, we and the years of worms between us. A boy, as Glen had promised: huddled close around his death, laid down with his knees drawn up tight against his chest to make him dog-sized, make him fit the grave. He still had rags of skin and flesh and tendon, as the dog did; he still had rags of clothing also. His trainers had survived the worms, as had his nylon jacket. The rest was shreds and patches.

'There's a tarpaulin in the bag, Dan,' Blake said. 'Lay that out, and let's see if we can lift him.'

'Why bother?' Henry asked. 'We've found him, okay; what are we going to do with him now? Cover him up again and leave him, that's my suggestion.'

'Henry, we've got to find out who he is. Give him back to his family, Glen said…'

Henry's face suggested that we'd done enough for Glen already, and too much perhaps. 'We could give the police a tip, let them come and fetch him.'

'And let them find what we can't, some clue to lead them back to Glen? No way. We'll do this ourselves, as anonymous as we can make it…'

I thought we'd end up dumping bones in a box on someone's doorstep. Not pretty, but we'd done ugly things before. I'd do anything, I thought, to make these last days easier for Glen. Never mind how hard they were for the rest of us. There was a debt, our bright and shining tiger-years, we owed them all to him. Now in his grey descent, he could ask more and far more than this.

When we got back to his place, he wasn't asking anything. Like consciousness, lucidity came and went in tides, as though there really were a lunar link; he could be aware, he could be self-aware, but the rhythms of both were different and they were rarely in sync one with the other.

Tosh didn't want to see what we'd brought back with us, and no blame to him for that. I didn't want to see it myself, in the bright garage-light where Blake was laying it out on a pasting table, like a makeshift morgue. Plenty of space in there, we'd long since got rid of Glen's old car. We had joint power of attorney, all six of us; Tim had fixed that six months before, when we made this pact with Glen. He wasn't dead yet but his estate was ours none the less to keep or sell, to divide up as we chose. I'd thought his car, his house, his books would be the most of our responsibilities; I hadn't thought we might take possession of his history, his skeletons, the bodies he'd left in his burning wake.

I hadn't known there were any literal bodies, though it didn't come as too much of a shock. Thinking about it, looking back, I was only surprised that all six of us survived him in the one sense, as he had been then, and again that we would all survive him in the other sense, that he would be the first of us to die. *The Seven Sisters* they used to call us, we used to call ourselves, but he was always more than elder sister and guiding light. Devil, tempter, bully, scourge – all of those and more, he whipped us wild and we were too young to do anything but dance manically at his heels, spinning faster, skidding further, desperate to outdo him if only to show that we could do it too. Boys did die, then as now; one of us surely should have died, perhaps we all deserved to. It seemed bizarre sometimes that it was Glen who was dying now, before any of us had had the chance to nip ahead of him. He always used to lead the way, but he'd had intuition or seemed to, he always seemed to know just where to stop...

No great surprise, though, that another boy had died, a greater sacrifice. I was only shocked that I didn't know, that none of us knew. I slid my hand beneath Glen's, and gazed reluctantly into his eyes. When he was truly living, when he was light they were gravity, blue and potent, blinking at nothing; now they glittered dully, crazed and smeared, frantic behind a veil of murk. He was blind, we thought, as near as we could tell; for sure he didn't see us, nor anything we tried to show him. In losing sight or just forgetting how to see, it seemed that he'd forgotten how to blink also, or else lost sight of the point of it. His tear-ducts were dry, his fund, his reservoir exhausted; we bathed his eyes to keep them moist, to soothe them.

Trying to soothe him if he should need it, if those trapped and frantic eyes weren't doubly deceptive, saying no more than they saw, I gave him senseless words to match his senselessness: 'It must be a weight off your mind, my love, that must have been some burden to carry all these years...'

I didn't think Glen had carried it at all except as a fact, one little historical detail, a truth that he remembered: *I killed a boy and buried him in the hills, Daniel knows where.* He'd left it to us to carry, as we carried him now and the ever-increasing weight of him, as we'd carry his coffin between the convenient six of us when he was dead. I thought Glen might even have planned that. Perhaps that was why we none of us had died, he'd known that he would need us at the end.

*

As it turned out the boy wasn't hard to name, and only a little harder to identify. He'd carried a purse in his jacket, in a zipped inner pocket; it was barely marked, despite the years of rotting. Inside the purse was a cashpoint card.

'Mr D B Tunnicliffe,' Henry read out, holding the card between fastidious fingers which had been scrubbed and disinfected like my own, like everyone's; dirty boys once, we'd all learned to be scrupulously clean. 'Mean anything to anyone?'

We played with the name, the initials, as we would have done before. D B – Dirty Boy, Dust Bin, Dave Brubeck, Dandelion & Burdock? Dog's Breath, Dog's Breakfast? (*Dog's Body*, but I kept that to myself.) Tunnicliffe – Tunk, Tuna, Tuna Fish? Tinkerbell, if the kid had been a fairy…?

Nothing tinkled any of our bells, though. Henry slipped the card into a pocket of his suit, and said he'd make enquiries.

Took him less than twenty-four hours. The following evening, we had the lad all lined up, named and tagged and wrapped up, ready to return.

Derek Brian Tunnicliffe, according to his records: seventeen years old when his account fell into disuse, presumably around the same time that he fell into that dark hole on the moor. Not living at home, not officially employed, not in a steady relationship (amazing, the details that banks record), he seemed to have been gone a while, a lag of a few weeks between the last transaction on his account and the police putting him down as a missing person. Even then, they seemed to have done little more than fill in the paperwork. One more gay boy skipping town, and so what? He might have been running from his dealer, his pimp, one of his clients, anyone. Happened all the time: boys came, boys went, it made no difference. They all looked the same to the law.

Seven years later – exactly on the first day they were allowed to – his parents applied to have him rendered officially dead. More paperwork, no passion, and the account was closed. Records had only been kept this long, Henry said, because of the unusual circumstances, against the remote chance of his returning. Officially dead didn't necessarily mean defunct, and his bank was covering its back as banks do, Henry said, the world over.

He sounded as though he approved. In this case, so did I. We had the parents' last-known address, we could dump the bones in a cardboard box and give them back their boy, however little they wanted him.

Except that I didn't want to. That was what Glen had asked and all that he had asked: a local habitation and a name, find out who he was and give him back. He hadn't suggested going further. Well, he wouldn't, would he? He'd known the truth himself, necessarily; if he'd felt no need to share it over all these years, why should he want it shared around now, even if he could remember? He wanted the ends tied off and tucked away, nothing more than that.

I wanted more, and didn't believe I was alone. I used to follow Glen without question, but no longer. *How?* and *Why?* were beacons blazing in my head, and the man who had the answers neither would nor could tell me now. We had a tame GP to supervise our nursing, but he wasn't really one of us. We couldn't take him to the garage, show him bones and ask him to tell us *how* the kid had died, stabbed or strangled, what; I doubted his ability in any case. I thought a specialist with a lab at his disposal might have thrown his hands up in defeat. There was too little flesh remaining to give any easy reading, and we'd hacked the bones about despite our care, as we dug them out. Blake and Henry between them had done more, washing the mud away while I'd sat with Glen, likely washing off a putative scientist's last chance.

Why was another matter, and we had perhaps some hope of working that out. Gifted the boy's full name, Tim remembered

91

him, and prompted memories in the rest of us. Glen had loved Python, so we had too; we'd called the kid Brian, with a giggling tag-line, *he's not the Messiah, he's a very naughty boy...*

More than naughty, he'd been a sinner by our lights. Good boys steal, of course they do, but never from their mates. Brian had been compulsive, unless he was simply stupid. When he was around – in bars, in clubs, at parties; jealous of our own company, we'd kept him at what distance we could manage – we were always careful to keep a hand on our purses and an eye on our bags. At a gig one time I'd been dancing, I'd stripped off a favourite silk shirt to sweat half-naked under the lights, under the beat; when I went to cool off, the shirt was gone from where I'd left it. Next time I saw Brian, he was wearing it.

Compulsive or not, he was definitely stupid. I took the shirt back, left him with bruises for a finder's compensation. Any bright kid would have taken the lesson with the lumps, and been grateful. You needed to be bright to survive that world we lived in then; when Brian vanished, I guess some of us wondered if maybe he'd been dimmer than we knew, if he'd turn up in the river one night with bad drugs in his blood or worse than bruises on his body. Both had happened before, both would happen again. When you took yourself to market the way we did every night, you needed to be part of a conglomerate, you needed at least one buddy to watch your back. Brian was always peripheral, always alone.

Now we were wondering if maybe it had been a different story, though the ending was the same: if the little toad had wangled his way into Glen's house, and tried to make off with something. Glen had always been protective of his assets. My shirt had cost Brian a serious beating; it took little imagination to write that just a little larger, to remember Glen's temper and his sheer physicality, the strength those extra years had given him...

'What I don't get, though,' I said slowly, 'if that's what

happened, if he laid into the jerk and Brian died, then okay, he thought he'd bury the body and stick a dog on top of it in case anyone saw the disturbed earth and came to check, fine – but why drag me into it, why make me dig the grave, or start it? Why make such a ritual of it, something I was bound to remember?'

'That's easy,' said Henry, as Tim had before him. Smart boys, these professionals. 'He was setting you up. Glen could lie for England, but not you. That's why you got a record, Dan, while the rest of us stayed clean; your face is like a signed confession. Anyone came asking questions about a grave on the moor, you'd blush and stammer, give yourself away without saying a word. It'd be clear as day that you knew something, where it was at least. That would've been enough. You remember what the cops were like back then, go for an easy target and fit him up if need be, if they couldn't find the proof. And Glen knew you'd say nothing, he'd be safe…'

I shook my head, more a plea than a refusal. 'He wouldn't do that. Not to me.'

'Why not? You didn't have fifteen years of history together, not back then. You were the last of us to join up, remember, the last one Glen found. He probably hadn't known you six months, you certainly weren't a fixture yet. Why would he give you a break? He used us all, Dan, you know that.'

And was using us still, and we still let it happen. That was the hold he had, the debt we owed. Henry was right, of course, I'd never have grassed him up; I'd have served his time if I had to and thought myself a martyr for the doing of it, thought it a far, far better thing than ever I'd done before…

Even so it was a cold picture that Henry painted, a banker's view of the world, investments and returns and selling short. I didn't want to believe it; neither, I thought, did the others.

Lord, I believe; help thou mine unbelief. Please? Make it flourish, make it strong…?

In pursuit of that, perhaps, I urged them all to do some

serious thinking, to drum up whatever memories they could. We'd been living half in that world anyway for months now, back in orbit around Glen again as we had not been for years; we carried it with us daily, and fresher every day. There must be more stories about Brian, someone surely must have spent more time with him than I had; he was a toe-rag, but a persistent toe-rag. A barnacle, even – as witness how he was clinging still, despite being fifteen years dead. Any little thing might help…

Myself, I went to sit with Glen a while, to talk him through this latest revelation. Had nothing back from him besides his nerve-less stare – he was failing fast now, the doctor said he'd likely not pull himself back to proper consciousness again – but I didn't mind that. I was scared, I think, of what he might say if he could get a grip on what I was telling him. *Yes, Daniel, it's true, you were my fall-guy if I needed one…* Or worse, perhaps, he might deny it and I'd never believe him now. It was true, he was a born deceiver. His greatest gift was to lie by misdirec-tion, to let drop a word or two and watch how people misconstrued him. I used to envy that so much, trapped as I was in my own directness, where I said *no* and my whole body said *yes, that's right, officer, take me away…*

In the end I took myself away, I left Glen to Blake's more prac-tical care and went home, went to bed. Stayed away all the next day, losing myself in my own memories, rebuilding us in my head the way we used to be, less brightly shining now, more tawdry in perspective; and was woken the morning after by a phone-call, early.

'Dan, it's Jody. I'm at Glen's.' Of course he was at Glen's; it was his watch. I didn't need to check the rota, I knew it by heart, and I wasn't on until that evening. For a moment I thought this was the call we were all waiting for, all dreading, *he's on his way, come now if you want to say goodbye.* But Jody went on, 'Tim's supposed to take over, I have to be early at work today; and he hasn't turned up, and his wife doesn't know where he is, he didn't come home last night. Can you stand in for him?'

'On my way,' I said wearily. I was the one among us who didn't work, at least not nine-to-five; hence I was the one among us who got these calls day or night, the permanent standby as well as a regular lead.

Never before for Tim, though. Tim was the guy who lived his life to a metronomic standard, who was always where he should be when he said he'd be there. For Tim not to show was disturbing; if his wife Lisa couldn't find him, that made it serious. I wanted to say *call the hospitals, call his office, call the police,* but she'd have done all that already.

I got to Glen's sooner than Jody had expected me, largely by virtue of not showering, not cleaning my teeth, forgoing coffee and turning up in yesterday's clothes, if any of those are virtuous. Virtue must be relative, I guess.

'How is he?'

'Quiet.'

I nodded. That was what they'd told me on the phone yesterday, so I was more or less prepared when I looked into the room we'd set up for him on the ground floor, back in the days when he was still occasionally mobile but couldn't manage the stairs any more. He lay quite still in his high hospital bed; someone had persuaded his errant eyes to close, and I couldn't see the least movement in the sheet that covered him, I couldn't see his breathing.

'Glenda, love...'

I licked my finger and laid it lightly on his upper lip, felt the faintest touch of air. The doctor had warned us about this, had said that he could slip into a coma at any time and linger maybe for days before he died. He hadn't eaten for a while now; we had a drip going into his arm, enough to keep him comfortable, pain-free, hydrated, not enough to keep him alive. He'd said he didn't want that. 'When the time comes, let me go,' he'd said.

Well, we would. Slowly, reluctantly, but we would.

I sat in the chair beside his bed, put my hand on top of his and found the fluttering pulse that lingered there. Like a bird on a wire, like smoke in a breeze, it gave not the least promise of permanence.

Well, no more could any of us. If the most solid, the most settled, the most reliable of us could fail wife and friends and solemn oath and all – hey, we're all friable under pressure, it's the human condition. Glen had his pressures, we had ours. I wondered what Tim's were, beyond the ticking of a mortal clock: *time presses* was one of his most lawyer-like catch-phrases, I'd heard it a hundred times this year and we'd all watched the truth of it being acted out on Glen's body. I wondered if that was the problem, if he'd suddenly reached his limit, simply couldn't bear to witness these last days, the end of a long song.

And didn't believe it, couldn't make that coalesce with what I knew of Tim. Besides, even if he wanted to run out on us, why would he run out on his wife also? It didn't add up. So instead, inevitably, I wondered if there might be a connection with what else was new, a boy's body brought to light and laid out in the garage.

Tim had always been the focused one among us, the one who could party tonight but still keep an eye on tomorrow. For a while all he was looking for tomorrow was another party, but that changed. Quite suddenly he signed up for a college course, and then university after; while we dossed, he studied. He'd still come cheerfully to market with the rest of us, selling himself along with an acid chaser for the extra cash, but renting wasn't a career-choice any longer, it was just a way to supple-ment his grant and have some fun along the way. Inevitably, he found other ways to have fun, in other company; it wasn't much of a surprise to me when he faded away after he'd qualified, after he'd got his first job. Nor when he turned up again, only to invite us to his wedding.

It was always going to be Henry who missed him most. Those two had been the closest among us, the ones who seemed almost enough for each other until Tim started reaching further, the ones who didn't really need to follow Glen. Once Tim was gone, I watched with a kind of cynical amusement as Henry aped his journey into respectability. Not into marriage, never that: but first he got a daylight job as a bank clerk, then he started taking courses – to improve his prospects, he said, to advance his career – and before long we never saw him except in a suit and tie, even around the clubs.

Those of us who were left had settled slowly into other lives, the way you have to as entropy sets in, as the fire starts to cool. We were all of us cooler now, fallen out of orbit and *fear no more the heat o' the sun*: Glen was a vast red giant, all-engulfing and all but entirely burned out, too close to collapse. Swallowed within his dimness, his gravitational suck, it was hard to remember quite how brightly we'd burned.

One of us, though – I thought one of us must have flared once at least like a sun through a lens, to make a blister-point all unnoticed while the rest of us danced our wild wasteful scatter…

Henry came to relieve me, on time and in character, the button-down banker; half-drowning in *nostalgie de la boue*, I made a mad effort to see him as he used to be, short and skinny and fiery in orange jeans, glitter in his hair and his mascara. Hopeless; only the height remained, or the lack of it. Otherwise he was like the rest of us, a victim of the ever-turning world.

I fetched coffee and whisky and a second chair, so that we could both sit with Glen while we talked.

'I don't think it was Glen killed Brian,' I said bluntly.

'No?' His frown made his cheeks pudge out to emphasise the weight he'd accumulated, his hard-won gravitas. 'How not? He sent us to the body…'

'Oh, he knew, he must have helped to bury him. After he'd killed the dog for cover – and yes, all right, after he'd set me up. Double indemnity.' This might not be the first time Brian had been laid out in his garage; they must have stored the body somewhere until I'd done the spadework, the groundwork, laid the dog down in the first instance for them to slide Brian beneath. 'But I think he's doing the same thing again, only setting himself up this time. If the story leaks, it can't hurt him, how could it?' Henry was shaking his head; I said, 'Look. If one of us had killed Brian, for whatever reason, skip over that for now – what would he do? Back then? We were kids, remember. When we needed help, where did we run to? Every time?' To the source, inevitably: to the mythmaker, to the guiser, to Glen.

Now he was nodding, not following me, trying to skip ahead. 'You think – Tim? You think that's why he's vanished, in case it all came out?'

Oh, he was quick. Quick with his sums, at least, though he had no imagination. I almost smiled, as I said no. 'No,' I said softly, 'not Tim. Think about it. Brian was a thief; what could he ever have stolen that Tim would give a fuck about? Tim didn't care. He knew where he was going, and how to get there. Nothing else mattered, not to him. There was only one of us who was desperate to hang on to what he'd got.' I gave him a moment, then went on, 'What did he steal from you, Henry? What was so important, Brian had to die?' When he didn't answer, I added, 'There's only the three of us here, and Glen's not listening. No hidden tapes, I'm not wired for sound. Trust me.'

That far, I thought he would. And I was right. He sighed; he sipped in rotation, glass and mug; he looked at me and said, 'Brian was stealing my life.'

'Explain?'

'It was watching Brian that made Tim think about the way we were, the way we'd end up. Dead or addicted, or scavenging on the margins. The rest of us were too busy to look that far, or too stupid, or else just dazzled by Glen, thinking we could all be like him. Small chance of that, he was the exception; and even then he was only a survivor. Everyone's a survivor, until they lose it.' One rapid glance aside, to show me just how badly Glen had lost it in the end. 'Tim wanted better than that. It was Brian that drove him, every day; he used to tell me so, *Brian's my criterion*, he'd say, *it's Brian who makes me work to get away. I could be Brian so easily, we all could, we're halfway there already...* And he was right, I knew that, but I didn't care. I was young, I liked what we had and I wanted to keep it, I wanted to keep it all. Tim too, Tim especially. If I lost him, I knew I'd lose you all sooner or later, and likely soon. I wasn't ready for that. So I thought, if I got rid of Brian, Tim might lose his impetus and we could all go on as we were...'

And when it didn't work, when Brian's disappearance was a spur if anything, he cut his losses and went after Tim, rather than cling on to what was already fraying. He didn't need to say that, I understood him all too well.

I sat and watched him drain his glass, put down his mug; I watched him stand and walk away, I listened to the door close behind him and his car start in the street outside.

There were questions I hadn't asked him, but again I didn't need to. *Whose idea was it, to line me up as fall-guy at need?* Glen's, it must have been; Henry didn't have the imagination.

More importantly, *where's Tim?* – but I knew where to find Tim, if I chose to go looking. Again, Henry had no imagination. He'd use Glen's old tricks one more time, double indemnity, once he'd seen the danger. Tim had to go for fear of what he might remember, how many times he'd talked about Brian and what Henry had said in response. He was too lawyerly to let the memory slip, for old times' sake; he might not betray Glen, but no one else was safe. Usefully, he could be set up in his absence, with his absence. And if that pointing finger failed, he could still be hidden where people would stop looking before they got that far. For Glen's sake, *give him back to his family*, I thought I might write a postcard to the police. With gloves on, not to give hostages to fortune. I thought I'd tell them to go dig on the moor – where it was easy, freshly turned, not too hard a labour for an unfit man – and when they turned up a dog's bones they should just keep digging deeper, however hard the soil had been stamped.

It seemed as though I had a night watch now, to follow my long day. I poured myself another slug of whisky, turned to Glen – and found that Henry had turned thief despite Tim's care that he should not. He'd stolen from me the one thing I'd been hoarding, what I'd worked for all these months.

Glen was gone and I'd missed the moment, the chance to see him off. Only the weight of him remained, star-stuff without a hint of shine.

Stuart Pawson

ULTRA VIOLENT

There's a saying about a man needing to do three things in his lifetime before he can feel fulfilled. Trouble was, he couldn't remember them. 'Father a son' was almost certainly the first one, but the others had gone. Something about planting a tree or ploughing a field, perhaps? Ah well, it would give him something to think about as he lay on the sunbed, before he started the serious planning.

The eight-tube, high-output sunbed had been a good buy, he decided. It was Aristotle Onassis who said that the first essential for being successful was a tan, and he didn't do too badly for himself, did he? His first wife, the opera singer, wasn't anything special, but Jackie Kennedy was. Once his tan was up, he thought, he'd fetch the Bullworker down from the loft, start working out again. But seriously, this time.

He examined his reflection in the big mirror on the wardrobe door, looking for evidence of colour-change. There were red patches on his shoulders and knees, and his back itched where he couldn't see it, so it must be working. He raised the leg of his boxer shorts for a before-and-after comparison. Yes! No doubt about it – there was a difference!

He hated boxer shorts. These had little Santa Clauses on them, interspersed with sprigs of holly. He'd bought them for when he went to spend last Christmas with Auntie Joan, hoping that they'd create some amusement when he finally bedded his cousin Jennifer. Good lovers always have a sense of humour, he'd read in one of his magazines. It hadn't come to that, though, and the hilariously funny shorts had remained within the perpetual darkness of his cavalry twills. Jennifer liked him, he was sure. Maybe even fancied him. But he'd gone at a bad time, before her exams, and she was studying hard every night, round at her friend's house. Next time it would be different.

Thirty minutes front, thirty minutes back, the instructions said. Not a second more. He made sure the goggles were tight, flicked the timer fully over and slid under the ultra-violet tubes as they popped and flickered into life. He'd decided to wear the shorts under the sunbed so that later there would be a contrasting line showing next to his new Speedo swimming trunks, when he started going to the baths at the sports centre.

They were wrong about the three steps a man had to take to fulfilment. For a start, he hated children. The sex bit would be OK, but the skill was to avoid having kids. You only had to go down to the precinct to see how easy it was to have them. And any idiot could plant a tree. Trees would plant themselves quite happily, if humans didn't interfere. As for ploughing a field, it was hard to imagine anything more boring than driving in slow-motion circles until it was done. Yes, they'd definitely got it wrong.

And, of course, the most important one had gone unsaid. Why did men join the army? Why did Americans, even the women, carry fancy little handguns and then wander, late at night, into areas where they shouldn't go, secretly hoping that a mugger would dare to try it with them? Why were the SAS everybody's heroes?

He knew why. When you looked into your own mind, followed the tunnel right to the end, kicking aside all the junk that countless teachers and priests and probation officers had piled up along the way, not to mention parents and set books and hymns and all that crap, you came to a stone. A big flat stone, lying face down. He'd made the journey, dumped the debris, found the stone, dared to turn it over. The message underneath was simple. It said: A man is not a man until he has killed someone.

The click of the timer switching off startled him, and the temperature started to drop. He reached out, turned it back to maximum and rolled over, to go through his plan to commit the perfect murder. That would be the finishing touch in the re-invention of himself. After that he would have the inner confidence, the serenity, plus that indefinable air of mystery, to go with his new physical appearance. Two hundred miles was the magic distance. Drive two hundred miles, kill someone you'd never met before, drive home without leaving a trace behind. Easy. You'd be safer than a doctor at an inquest.

Sunday he polished the car. He'd bought it two weeks ago – a second-hand Ford Escort – and was determined to keep it immaculate. Next week he would put his plan into operation. Tuesday was the ideal day, he had decided. Tuesday was the low point of the week for most people. Nothing ever happened on a Tuesday.

Ideally, he would have liked to have a conversation with a policeman. Ask him a few questions, test his theories, but he didn't know one socially and he could hardly breeze into the local nick and start asking questions about murder enquiries, could he? He threw the wash leather into the bucket and drove round to the filling station to top-up the tyres and the petrol tank.

Parked in the schoolyard was a huge articulated caravan, with the emblem of the local police force on the side. 'There's a thief about' said the posters showing a fleeing youth, and 'Don't let him get away with it. Call in for advice.' He decided to do just that, after he'd been to the garage. Car thieves worried him. They were lowlife; should be exterminated.

Fifteen minutes later he climbed the four steps that took him inside the caravan. 'Morning, Sir,' the policeman in charge of the exhibition greeted him, his voice filtered through a black moustache.

'Er, good morning.' He wandered around, looking at the

displays of photographs and charts, conscious of the policeman's eyes following him.

'Anything you need any help with, Sir?' the officer asked after a decent interval.

'No, not really. Well yes. I have an Escort, and was wondering...'

'Let me tell you what's available for cars. Top of the range are microchips...' He droned through his spiel, explaining about concealed electronic implants that cost more than the Escort was worth, about tracking devices and silent alarms. 'And finally,' the policeman concluded, 'we have these.' He held up what looked like a fat fibre-tipped pen.

'Oh, what's that?' the visitor asked.

'Secret marker pen. Simply write your postcode on every-thing that is removable, then, if it ever turns up amongst some stolen property we can identify it. It shows up under an ultra-violet light, but otherwise it's invisible. One pound fifty to you, Sir.'

'Gosh. Just your postcode?'

'That's right. A postcode identifies the owner to within ten or fifteen houses. After that, we knock on doors.'

'Right, I'll take one.' He retrieved his purse from the inside pocket of his parka and offered a fiver to the policeman.

'Thank you, Sir. I'll just find you some change.'

His confidence was growing. He felt he'd struck up a small rapport with the officer. 'Thank you.' He placed the coins in the purse. 'Have you been doing this long?'

The policeman blinked, taken by surprise. 'About six weeks,' he said, because he couldn't think of a reason not to.

'Just at weekends?'

'That's right. We're slowly working our way round the county.'

'It's a good idea,' he told him, encouragingly. 'So you're a proper policeman the rest of the week?'

'Yes. Traffic.'

He noticed that the 'Sirs' were absent from the last few exchanges. 'Do you prefer being with Traffic to, say, catching murderers?' he asked.

The velcro moustache was decidedly down-turned at the ends. 'A death's a death, *Sir*,' the policeman told him, the *Sir* laid on like cheap margarine. 'And for every homicide in this country there are ten fatalities on the road.'

A young woman with two children clumped into the caravan. 'Right,' he agreed. 'OK.' He waved the pen. 'Thanks for this.' Cocooned in the Escort again, he threw the secret marker into the glove compartment and embraced the steering wheel, his body shaking with silent laughter. 'What a plonker!' he giggled to himself. 'What a flipping plonker!'

Tuesday, he drove north. The A1 took him into Yorkshire, and when he had 210 miles on the trip recorder, with the signs indicating Leeds off to the west, he took a slip road and headed east. It was agricultural land, with areas of woodland and still plenty of hedgerows. He drove methodically, turning on to narrower lanes as they occurred, looking for the ideal spot.

A Citroën estate was parked in a bald patch of ground at the edge of a wood. It was an unofficial car park for people out for a walk. Or dumping rubbish, his eyes told him, as he scanned the scattered bin liners and their spilled contents.

A dog, a nondescript terrier, came bounding towards the Citroën and then turned expectantly, waiting for his master to appear. He was middle-aged, wearing a chain-store padded coat and carrying a stick for the dog to chase. The man changed his shoes and opened the rear hatch to let the dog in, like he probably did every day, unaware that on this occasion he was being watched. 'Perfect,' the observer whispered to himself, noting the exact time. 'Just perfect.'

One week later, but two hours earlier in the day, he did the long drive north again. It was a bind, but that was the whole point.

Most murderers are careless, can't be bothered travelling too far. They work on their own doorsteps, and pay the penalty. The police mark the places where the bodies are found on a big map, and the killer almost always lives somewhere in the middle.

The next time – and he was sure there would be a next time – he'd come up here again, but to somewhere different. This first one would be put down to a random killing, but when there had been two or three… He'd have to wait, of course. A year would be about right. Not exactly a year; more like eleven months, or fourteen. Unpredictable, that was the key.

He felt good, seeing the world about him with a renewed clarity. There were voices, a choir, singing in his head. Last night he had purified himself. A man was about to die by his hands, so it was only right that he should be in a state of grace when he performed the act. He'd had beefburger steak and egg for tea; the meat to signify death, the egg for new life. *His* new life. He wouldn't eat again until it was over. Then he did the colonic irrigation, to rid his body of toxins, followed by ten minutes meditation. After that he watched videos of famous serial killers from his collection, nodding approvingly at their deeds, shaking his head and smiling at their mistakes, until he knew he was ready.

He parked the Escort in a gateway to a field about two hundred yards from the unofficial car park. A week earlier, after the man in the Citroën had departed, he'd made a reconnaissance of the area, studied the lie of the land. He knew exactly where the act would take place. From the boot he removed a long bundle wrapped in a blanket. He extricated the shotgun that had belonged to his step-grandfather and opened a brand new box of cartridges. Fifteen minutes later he concealed the gun under a bush in the hedgerow, alongside the path the man had to take, and waited.

So far, he'd been detached, almost clinical, and had marvelled at his own coolness. But as soon as the intended victim hove into view something else took over. He breathed deeply, controlling his excitement. Not for a single second did he doubt that he would do it. Today was the day that he would move onto a loftier plane than that inhabited by the fools and no-hopers that plagued his everyday life. Today he would play with the gods.

When the man was twenty yards away he stepped from the bushes, the gun held behind him. The man hardly noticed him, then smiled a greeting. At ten yards he levelled the shotgun. A puzzled look crossed the man's face, as if to say: 'Look here, you shouldn't wave that thing about.' At five yards he braced the butt into his body and stiffened his grip. At three he pulled the trigger.

The dog was leaping around the prostrate body, yapping and whining, so he shot that, too. Then he dragged the pair of them off the path and concealed them in the undergrowth, where they wouldn't be seen by passers-by, but would soon be discovered by a search party, after the alarm was raised. But by then he would be a long way away.

He found his way back to the car through the woods, ready to drop the gun into the undergrowth should he meet anyone else, but he didn't. The car started instantly, removing his last major worry, and he slipped the gear lever towards first and eased the clutch. The gateway was rutted where tractors had removed the harvest a few weeks earlier. The rear wheels of the Escort slid sideways into the depression and he sideswiped the gatepost.

'Hell!' he cursed, then remembered he had front-wheel drive and pulled out into the lane. A quarter of a mile later he stopped. There had been a murder somewhere in the Midlands a few years earlier, and he'd just remembered how the murderer was caught. He'd left flakes of paint from his car on the branch of a bush. The police identified the make and the model from the paint, and many months later an alert copper with not enough to occupy his mind had noticed a car of the right type with a scratch at exactly the right height. He shook his head sympathetically. That was bad luck, but he wasn't going to rely on luck. He climbed out to look for damage.

The bodywork was unmarked, but the rear wheel trim was partially dislodged and would have fallen off in the next few miles. He was calm, thinking rationally. Professional, that was the word. The trims were nothing special, not even the original ones fitted by Ford, and one found down the road half a mile from a body could hardly be considered a clue. There was even a spare one in the boot, so he wouldn't have to buy a new one. He kicked the trim back onto the wheel and was opening the car door when a thought occurred to him. It wouldn't be much of a lead to the police, but there was a way that it could be a *mis-lead*. A colossal mis-lead. He grinned at the thought of it, and congratulated himself on his clear thinking. Already he was in that lofty place where the eagles flew but the turkeys never ventured. It would always be like this from now on.

During the planning of the murder he had wondered about providing a red herring to direct the police down a wrong avenue, but had eventually dismissed the idea as an unnecessary complication. 'KISS' said the poster on the hospital notice board – Keep It Simple, Stupid. But one of the marks of greatness was the ability to adapt to changing circumstances; to be constantly updating the action plan. This was one of those times.

He took the secret marker pen from the glove compartment, where it had lain since he purchased it, and opened the Escort's boot lid. Wearing his driving gloves, he scrupulously cleaned every possible vestige of a fingerprint from the spare wheeltrim. Then, working right-handed, which was unnatural for him, he wrote a Leeds postcode in small figures near the inside edge of the trim. He knew Leeds was LS, so he wrote LS15, making it look as if it could be 16, followed by a 7 that might be a 1 and a WN that could have been almost anything. He drove back to the gateway and left it propped against the post he'd hit. After a comprehensive look around he drove away for the final time.

He'd done it! He donned his Ray-Bans for the drive home, towards the afternoon sun. It was going to be all sunshine from now on. The engine of the Ford purred effortlessly as he cruised down the A1, well inside the speed limit, singing along with the tunes on Radio 2. During a lull in the music he did an impression of a country bobby saying, 'We think the killer lives locally,' and giggled at his own joke until he had to find a tissue to blow his nose.

Next day he put the car through the car wash. At home he polished it until it hurt his eyes, paying extra attention to the wheels, removing every grain of foreign dirt from them. To a forensic scientist dirt was as distinctive as a fingerprint, so it was important to get rid of it all. On a whim, while the trims were off, he secret-marked them inside with his own postcode, using his proper hand and bigger, sloping letters and numbers.

After lunch he had a sunbathe. Maybe tomorrow, if he looked brown enough, he would consider visiting the swimming baths. It was relaxing on the bed, the warmth from the UV lamps penetrating the skin, reaching deep into his bones. God, he felt good. Eleven months was a long time to wait before he did it again. Maybe he'd have a rethink about that.

Thirty minutes front, thirty minutes back. That was the maximum safe dose. As the lamps clicked off after the hour, he was wondering how soon the police up in Yorkshire would examine the wheel trim under a UV lamp. First of all, they'd test it for fingerprints, but they'd find nothing there. Experts would check the size and manufacture, and find that it could have come from any one of ten million cars. No problem in that department. Then they would examine it for any dirt that might lead them to its original location, but again they'd draw a blank. It might be a day or two before they tested it in ultra-violet light.

Ultra-violet, he thought! Just like his sunbed. Would the secret marker pen show up under his sunbed? He quickly dressed and went out to the car. Two minutes later he was back in his bedroom, armed with one of the wheel trims. He fitted the goggles to his eyes and wound a few minutes on to the timer. The tubes, still warm, instantly burst into life. He bent over, holding the trim underneath them. Something was there, but it was indistinct. He raised the goggles, defying the instructions that came with the bed, and squinted at the plastic disc.

Somewhere outside he heard a car stop and the double slam of its doors, but it hardly registered in his brain. And he never noticed his own post code that he'd neatly written near the edge of the trim, for all his attention was grabbed by the huge block capitals emblazoned across the middle, glowing like a neon sign. One letter, three numbers, three more letters. It was a registration number. His number. The number of the Escort, inscribed there by the previous owner. Outside, the hinges of his front gate squealed as it opened, and he heard the crunch of gravel underfoot as someone came to his side door. He sank to his knees, oblivious of the short-wave radiation burning into his retinae. What was it the plonker of a policeman had said? 'We're slowly working our way round the county.' That was it. And, more chillingly, 'After that, we knock on doors.' He turned around, waiting for the sound of knuckles against woodwork.

Ann Cleeves

SAD GIRLS

I shouldn't be here. OK, so they all say that. But with me it's true. You don't get a custodial with a first offence. Not if you plead guilty. Anyone'll tell you. That's what my solicitor said. Though when I got sent down he looked as if that's what he'd been expecting all the time. I don't know why he was there at all. It's not like he cared. When I saw him in the waiting room before it all started he didn't even recognise me and he didn't come down to see me after.

That morning in the Crown Court seems like a dream now. It did even then. Sometimes I lose it, get lost in the dreams. 'You're away with the fairies, you,' my Nan used to say. It was freezing outside, but sweltering in the court and something was humming, the central heating, or one of the strip lights packing up. I started thinking about a summer when we went for a picnic on Bidston Hill. It was dead hot that day too and there was the same sort of background noise, but I think that was insects, or wind in the grass, or electricity in the overhead cables. Then the judge started talking and I was jerked back to the court. It was like when you wake up suddenly. Everyone was looking at me, but even then it took me a minute to work out what he was saying.

'A betrayal of the worst possible kind... No alternative to custody...' He had a wheezy voice and I had to turn my head and strain to hear him. It was a big, high room and the words seemed to echo.

They took me down to the cells to wait for the van. I was

shaking. Scared of course but excited too, to tell the truth. Not many girls get sent to prison. And I'd seen that programme – *Bad Girls*. But this place is nothing like *Bad Girls*. There aren't any sexy officers and they don't screw the women. I mean, I wouldn't expect them to go for a fat slag like me, but nothing that thrilling ever happens here. All there is, is routine. Every fucking day the same. Same unlock time, same work, mopping the same patch of lino, same fucking corned beef sandwiches for tea.

If I'd wanted I could have gone on education. I did a test on reception and then there was an interview. We sat in a class-room with posters on the wall about reading. One picture was of a woman lying on a huge bed, which was covered with a leopard skin or something. She was wearing a silky nightie and reading a book. For some reason I couldn't stop looking at it. The teacher was alright too. Middle-aged but still smart. Decent hair-cut, good clothes. She had her key pouch tucked under her jacket and I like that. Some of them flaunt the keys. It's as if they're saying: You have to do what I tell you. I keep you locked up. I'm in charge. As if really they wish they were one of the screws, all dressed up in uniform and polished boots.

Mrs Jenner didn't talk like that. She had a gentle voice and she remembered I was deaf in one ear so she sat on my good side, and then close enough so she didn't have to talk loud. Close enough for me to smell the clothes she was wearing, washing-powder fresh, and that took me right back to my Nan's house in New Ferry, the washing on the clothes horse in front of the gas fire and condensation running down the windows and the little kids playing in the street outside.

'I'm looking for recruits for my New Start group,' Mrs Jenner said. It was an invitation. Relaxed and easy, but she really wanted me to be there. That's what it felt like. I really wanted to be there too. It would give me time away from the noise of the wing and if I sat next to Mrs Jenner I could smell her clothes again and hear her tired voice. But the girls had already told me about New Start. It was a group for dumb-asses. So I got a cleaning job instead. I've got a reputation to keep up. No one's going to call me thick.

I don't mind the reputation because it keeps the scum off my back, but I don't deserve it. Honest. The papers made a fuss about the assault on Mrs Barber. As if I battered her or some-thing. Well, I didn't. I took the job at Rose Bank because I like old people and they like me. That stuff in the papers was shite. I never realised before what lies they tell. There were sly comments about my weight too. They made me out to be a monster.

Angie, the new girl on the wing, isn't on remand like most of them. She's been sentenced like me and there's been stuff about her in the papers, even a picture of her running into court with a blanket over her head. Everyone was talking about her before she even got here, the screws as well as the girls, calling her all sorts. You could tell she was going to have a hard time. Sometimes I wonder if the papers were lying about her too. Not telling the whole truth at least. Not that I say anything. I make out I'm shocked like the rest of them. I wouldn't want the girls thinking I'm making excuses for her. What excuse is there for killing a baby? Your own baby.

She looks very young. Bad skin and blotchy eyes as if she hasn't slept for months, but somehow still a pretty face. When I saw her first she was getting hassle in the dinner queue. Nothing serious but she was close to tears. She looked up, straight at me, as if she expected me to help. But I didn't. I turned away and walked off. It makes me sick, the attention she's getting, the fuss she causes.

I get so bored in here, I could scream. Nan used to like wildlife programmes and I saw an elephant once on a film she was watching; this elephant tipped back its head, lifted its trunk and bellowed, so loud you'd think the noise would flatten trees. That's how I feel. That's how loud I want to scream. I'm not used to having so little to do. I've always worked, not like most of them in here. I got a job in McDonald's while I was still at school, then straight to the Old People's Home when I was sixteen. When I first went after the position the owner, Mrs Carruthers, wasn't sure.

'I don't know, dear. You're very young. We were hoping for someone with experience.' A West Kirby posh voice, but fake. You can always tell.

'I looked after my Nan.'

'So you said.' She looked at me over her glasses, wrinkling her nose in disgust and I was only a size 16 then.

Of course it wasn't the fact that I'd cared for my Nan which persuaded her. It was knowing I wouldn't have to be paid anywhere near the minimum wage until I was eighteen.

Rose Bank was a big, red-brick place with a high wall all round it and glass on the top to stop scallies getting in. There wasn't much of a garden. I don't remember any roses. Inside it was hot and airless and it stank of old people and talcum powder. I had a uniform, royal blue, with buttons up the front. It looked like a nurse's dress. I was proud of that. It's a proper job, isn't it, nursing? At the end I even had my own set of keys – one for the medicine cupboard and one for the front door – which I clipped to a loop on my belt. Mrs Carruthers was very strict about locking the front door. She didn't want any of them going walkabout. And it *was* like nursing, what I did, helping the residents up in the morning, onto the commode first, then washing and dressing them, putting them to bed at night.

Most of them were confused, so confused they didn't notice I was thieving from them. And if they didn't notice, what harm was there in it? Who would their money go to when they died? The sons and daughters who'd stuck them into Rose Bank to rot, that's who. Not the fat lass in the blue uniform who wiped their shitty bums.

I wasn't always fat. Now I'm the biggest woman on our wing. If I'm in the mood I make a joke of it. Walking down the corridor in full stride I shout, 'Out the way, yous, or I'll flatten ya.' No one else skits me about my size. They wouldn't dare. Not with my reputation.

When I was little I was skinny. I've seen the photos. You can see the bones under the skin. 'A walking X-ray,' my Nan called me. And always starving, always scrounging sweets off the kids at school, nicking fruit from the market. That's all I can remember of the time before I went to stay with my Nan, being hungry and hiding from Danny, my step-dad.

Angie, the girl who killed her baby, is thin. Not X-ray thin like I was. Maybe a size 10. Little tits and no flesh on her bum. I watch her. She's not eating. She picks at her food then throws it away. I know she's screwed up but she's not helping herself. She talks about the baby. That's really dumb. It upsets the girls, especially them with kids on the out, and it doesn't show respect. Part of me wants to put her right. For her own good. I want to say to her: Stop bringing attention to yourself, you stupid cow. The red eyes and the crying all night, and the demanding to speak to a Listener, none of that will help. The same part of me wants to comfort her. I imagine what it would be like to put an arm around her shoulder and to say: Tell *me* about the baby. I'll be your very own Listener. I want to help. But I don't do that. Because then the other girls would think I'd gone soft, or I was a lezzie, or something. And because part of me feels sick to the stomach about what she did. Do you know how she killed her baby? She starved it to death. She didn't feed it or change it. She just left it in a cot with a blanket on it, like it was a doll or something. Until it was too weak even to cry. And it's not like Angie's a stupid tart. She's doing IT in education. Before she fell pregnant she worked in an office. You wouldn't have caught *her* wiping old ladies' arses.

I worked at Rose Bank for four years before I was caught. That was because I'm not daft, even though they wanted me to do New Start, and I wasn't too greedy. I only took stuff from the inmates who were too disturbed in their minds to know what was happening, and then only if their relatives never visited. If Mrs Barber hadn't come in that day and seen me with her purse I'd still be there now. And even when I looked up from the dressing table and saw her standing in the doorway, her mouth open, dribbling a bit like she did when she got agitated, I wasn't worried. She'd had a stroke which affected her speech. Even if she could make the staff understand, none of them cared enough about her to listen. I was the only one there who was kind to her.

I said, 'It's alright, Mrs Barber. I've just brought the clean washing, love.'

They were supposed to get their own clothes back but they never did. That day there was a pair of pink knickers belonging to Miss Keating on the pile I'd put on Mrs Barber's bed.

I smiled at her. I'd found most of them would respond to a smile even if they were too crazy to take in the meaning of what you were telling them. But she walked towards me, a little arm like a twig raised above her head, as if she intended to hit me. The sleeve of her cardie was so loose that it slid back to her shoulder and I could see her elbow, all knobbly and grey. I panicked. I pushed her out of the way and it was like pushing a pile of twigs. She crumpled into a heap on the floor. I was already working out a story about how she'd fallen but it was too late for that. There was Mrs Carruthers, eyes fiery with triumph, not concerned for poor Mrs Barber, just enjoying the drama and the fact that she'd caught me out.

The solicitor advised me to plead guilty from the start. He sat across the table from me in the police station and pulled back his lips to smile, showing uneven yellow teeth.

'With your history you might even get probation. It is a first offence. Play it right in court. Look pathetic.'

He had a bald head and a ginger moustache with dandruff in it. I never knew moustaches could get dandruff. I imagined the bits of skin, like rows of ants, marching down his skull and over his ears, looking for somewhere else to go once the hair on his head started to fall out. I couldn't take him seriously after that. Anyway, it's hard to do pathetic when you're fourteen stone. And I must have played it wrong, mustn't I? Because the magistrates sent me to the Crown Court, and there on a freezing day, with the central heating buzzing, I got sent down. At least Nan wasn't around to read all that shite in the papers. She didn't have to listen to the neighbours gobbing on about where she'd gone wrong in bringing me up.

Nan gave me a home when the social took me into care, that last time, after Danny hit me so hard he burst the eardrum. *He* never got taken to court. Not enough evidence, the social said, and put 'failure to thrive' on the form my Mam had to sign. I never asked Nan about it. She had heart trouble and it wasn't good for her to get angry. One night though, not long before she died, she talked about it. She was just back from the club, full of barley wine, according to Rita Murphy next door, and collapsed in the chair by the fire, still with her coat on, her skirt all round her thighs.

'He threatened the daft tart from the Social,' she said. 'Nothing obvious, just letting her know he could find her if he had to. And that he knew where her kids were at school.'

But Nan was already ill by then, and pissed, and she always did like a good story.

I remember stuff like that when I'm mopping the floor. Mop, shift the metal bucket with my foot, rinse, wring and mop again. It doesn't take much concentration, even for a thicko like me. And I think about Angie who starved her baby to death. I can't get her out of my fucking head. Whatever I'm remembering, I always come back to a picture of her. She can do pathetic. That's how I think of her. Looking at me with those pathetic eyes. In Association, when they're showing the same soppy video they showed us a month ago, I talk to the other girls with a reputation to keep and we think of ways to teach Angie a lesson. It doesn't make me feel as good as I think it will, but I can't help myself. I won't be haunted by her.

There's no rule 43 here. Not like the men's nicks where they can sign onto a separate wing for their own safety, the wing where the beasts live, like it's some sort of zoo. We're women, too civilised for that.

Too subtle too. Women torture with words.

I'm only a New Start girl, but I know what that means.

Everywhere Angie goes there are whispers. I'm not part of it. I'm big and I'm obvious and the screws would be onto me at once. Glad of the excuse. They don't like me. They think I'm a monster and a batterer of old ladies. We set the good girls onto Angie. The library orderly and the hospital orderly and the pretty little thing from the kitchen. How could *they* refuse. Better to have me on their side. Much better.

Then Angie comes to see me. I'm in my pad. I'm on the bottom bunk because who'd want all that weight on top of them? Not reading or listening to my Walkman, just lying there, remembering. I open my eyes and there she is, hovering at the doorway, all spotty and pinched. The girls in the corridor must have let her through to me for a laugh. She's wearing prison gear – loose shapeless jeans and a sweat shirt that's been through the laundry so many times you can't tell what colour it was meant to be. Like the old people's clothes at Rose Bank.

'Make them stop,' she says.

'What's that, love?' I lift myself onto one elbow, squint at her, pretend I really haven't got a clue what she's on about.

'They'd listen to you.'

She's right. They would. And for a minute I'm tempted. It's a chance to be God. In here, which is the only world that counts, right now, I have real power.

She senses that I'm hesitating because she takes a few steps in. Tentative. Watching my face all the time for signs that I'm going to turn on her. Like I used to watch Danny when he had that mood on him.

'Please,' she says. 'I'd do anything.' And she sits at the end of the bunk. Not touching me. Just perching there, looking at me with the pleading face and the eyes red from crying. I could reach out and comfort her, as I've imagined. And that's what I want to do. But I can't because I'm not soft, and what would the other girls say? Where would my reputation be then?

'Sorry love,' I say. 'Don't know what you're talking about.'

I lie back and shut my eyes. She's so light that I don't feel her getting up from the bunk and there's so much noise on the wing outside that I don't hear her leave. When I open my eyes, she's gone.

The next thing I hear, she's dead. The news gets out as it always does. She hanged herself in her cell with photos of her little girl stuck all over the wall. Later that day Mrs Jenner asks to see me. She's still trying to get me into that group. Makes her look a tosser, I suppose, if there are no takers.

'Did you hear about Angie?' she asks.

I nod. 'What'll happen?'

'There'll be an enquiry. They'll say she shouldn't have been here. She was sick. She should have been in hospital. They'll write the things that always get written. "A young life wasted. So sad."' Her voice was more tired than I'd ever heard it. 'I can't tempt you then? With the group?'

A pause. 'No thanks, Miss. Not really my thing.'

The screw lets me out of Education and onto the wing. I sail down the corridor I clean every day. 'Look out, yous,' I shout. 'Or I'll flatten ya.'

But my heart's not in it.

Martin Edwards

THE CORPSE CANDLE

A few hours ago, I feared I would die before the night was out. Now all is quiet. We are alone with each other, and safe. I shall dare to tell you the story of the murders – but after tonight, I promise that you will never hear me speak of them again.

At least my father's passing was natural. I had cared for him, as well as my brother Owain, since we lost my mother when I was eleven years old. The farm was set in a scrap of pasture amidst the moorland, under the forbidding shadow of Foel Eryr. It took the efforts of all three of us to scrape a living and keep body and soul together. My father did his best to teach us what he knew. I am sure he realised that his time was short, for he was frequently unwell and often spoke of how we would cope after his passing. While Owain was to take charge of the farm, my father decreed that I should keep house. I suspect that my brother found the prospect as unappealing as did I. Owain had a sweetheart in Morfil, of whose existence my father was ignorant, and Kenedlon was a fiery woman who would have no wish to share her home with a spinster sister-in-law. For my part, I had no wish to spend the rest of my life as an unpaid drudge for a married couple.

Our life at the farm was not unrelieved gloom. The harshness of our existence was softened by those evenings when my father would call Owain and I together in front of the fire and recount stories that the two of us always found thrilling. Tales of the Otherworld, of mermaids and giants, of the little fair people and the Sunken Lands. The legends unlocked my imagination, and from an early age I repeated the stories to myself in bed, as I might do to a child of my own. All the while I was dreaming of a life far away from our humble farm, a life stocked to overflowing with miracles and untold riches.

A few weeks before my father's death I had a taste of freedom, when Owain took me to the market at St David's. My brother arranged this with my blessing. I was to be his alibi, so that he could conduct an illicit tryst with Kenedlon. I readily agreed to help him, since the trip gave me the opportunity, however briefly, to spread my own wings. The visit to St David's made me all the more determined to seize the chance to break away from the lower slopes of the Preseli Hills. That chance came all too soon. One chilly night at the end of May, my father started with a hoarse racking cough and within hours the first man I ever loved was dead.

'Rhiannon,' my brother said in a low voice after the funeral. 'Did you see the corpse candle?'

I stared at him. 'What are you talking about?'

'I saw it, sister,' he whispered. 'Just as father described it. You remember, surely? The sign that St David prayed for, so that people should be able to prepare themselves for a death?'

'I know the story, of course,' I said reluctantly. The only way to cope with our father's death, I had decided, was not to dwell upon it, but rather to think about anything other than the old man with the tender smile – and here was my brother, reminding me of our nights spent listening to him. 'The candle is seen passing along the route of a funeral, or hovering near the spot where someone is to die. But...'

'On the evening father took ill, a few hours before, I saw from outside a light in the room next to the kitchen. Because we so seldom use it, I was perturbed. Yet when I entered the house and hurried into the room, I saw no light.'

'Your mind was playing tricks,' I said. 'It was only a story, like that of the Water Horse of St Bride's Bay or the Mermaid at Aberbach.'

He shook his head with characteristic obstinacy. 'I know what I saw, Rhiannon. That room where I saw the light, it is the same room where we laid father to rest, when he was coughing so terribly and could not manage to reach his bed.'

'What's this?' a high-pitched voice demanded. 'Owain, shame on you! You are terrifying the poor girl!'

We had been joined by Kenedlon. She linked arms with Owain and I saw a proprietorial gleam in her hazel eyes. I felt a sudden spurt of sympathy for my brother. He was no match for her and I was reaffirmed in my determination to carve out a new life.

'The legend came true,' he said mulishly.

Kenedlon simply laughed and, with a flap of the hand in my direction, led her trophy away to be admired by her proud and stupid parents.

I did not waste time. My father had a cousin, Rhodri, who lived a little way outside Pembroke and within a week I persuaded him to offer me lodging at his farm in return for keeping his house. A few days later, when Rhodri was out in the fields, I walked into the centre of the town and found myself watching a procession of soldiers heading towards the castle.

That was the first time I saw Brochwel. In truth, it would have been impossible not to notice him. He was at the head of the procession, a tall and fearsomely dressed man, with long flowing hair and a beard. In comparison, his warriors appeared puny. I thought he resembled one of the giants my father had loved to describe. I could believe this man to be capable of the tremendous feats of strength recounted in legend, of tearing up trees or hurling the great stone from the summit of Freni Fawr to Llanfyrnach far below.

People kept running up towards him, calling out words of praise. For my part, I made no effort to conceal my admiration or my sense of awe. Our eyes met and his gaze lingered upon me. I did not shrink away, but rather luxuriated in his scrutiny. I felt the hotness of his gaze, could imagine him picturing what lay beneath my simple dress. My whole body tingled. Never in my life, not even during the excitement of my visit to St David's, had I known an experience such as this. It was as if at last I had cause to believe that dreams can indeed come true.

He paused for a moment, as if making up his mind. Then he gave me a quick nod before marching on, at the head of his troops. I turned to a wizened old woman who was standing beside me in the crowd.

'Who was that?' I asked innocently.

She treated me to a gap-toothed grin. 'Do you not know, my dear?'

'Would I need to ask the question if I did?'

'That is Brochwel.'

My mouth fell open. 'But…'

Her laugh reminded me of the cackling witches my father used to describe. 'Yes, my dear, I saw the way he looked at you. He is a man, after all. But more than that. He is a prince of Dyfed.'

'He is very handsome,' I said.

'Well, he is a fine figure of a man,' the old woman chuckled. 'And you know, he is not spoken for. His wife died last year and he has yet to return to the altar. His mistresses are two-a-penny, my dear, and you are so lovely. If you set your cap at him, he will not spare them a second glance.'

Her directness was startling, but I welcomed it. If she had set out to make me happy, she could not have succeeded better in her aim. I had no reason to doubt her honesty. She had, as she said, seen how he looked at me. With, I told myself – although still hardly daring to credit it – love in his eyes.

What to do next? I did not have to toss the question around in my mind for long. As I drifted away from the crowd, a young man accosted me.

'Excuse me, but I am Pryderi, cousin and aide to Brochwel of Dyfed. The prince has asked me to enquire your name.'

I studied him, trying to get his measure. 'And why does he

trouble to put the question?' I asked boldly.

'He says you will learn the answer tonight, in the castle hall.'

'I will?'

'Assuredly,' the young man confirmed. 'A feast is being held to celebrate my cousin's triumph in battle against the brigands from the north.'

'What if I am unable to attend?' I asked, greatly daring.

'Then you must cancel your engagement,' he said, with a seriousness that I found both comical and appealing. 'An invitation from a prince is not to be spurned.'

'Very well, I accept his invitation.'

My interlocutor allowed himself a smile. 'Thank you. And your name?'

'It is Rhiannon,' I said. To myself, I said: *Rhiannon and Brochwel.* Trying out the names together. The coupling had a certain charm.

Brochwel was waiting for me at the castle gate that evening. Hesitating in the street outside, I caught his eye and he beckoned me forward. As I approached, Pryderi, who had been standing at the prince's side, gave me a quick wave of greeting and then slipped away, leaving the two of us alone.

'Rhiannon,' Brochwel said simply. I liked his voice. It was deep and strong.

I bowed. 'My lord.'

'You will sit by my side at the feast.'

'I am honoured,' I said quietly. 'But I do not deserve the honour. There are many other women, far more worthy than…'

'Nonsense! You are the one whose company I seek.'

'I do not understand, my lord. You do not even know me.'

'I have seen you,' he said, 'and that is enough. You were watching the procession.'

At close quarters I was struck by the sheer size and physical power of the man. He was no longer young, but he was taller and broader than anyone I had ever known. I thought that he could with ease have picked me up in one hand. Even so, I was aware of an uncertainty inside the vast frame, a hidden weakness that few would even guess at.

'Celebrating your triumph,' I said.

He laughed, a sound like a thunderclap. Yet I guessed that, beneath his bravado, this strong man was unsure what to make of the teasing note that had entered my voice. 'You think me immodest, then, Rhiannon?'

I shook my head and spoke meekly. 'Not at all, my lord. You have vanquished your enemies, your people are devoted to you. You have earned your garlands.'

'So you think I have everything, do you, Rhiannon?'

I looked into his eyes. 'Surely, my lord?'

'I'm afraid I do not,' he said.

'Well,' I rejoined, my gaze unwavering. 'I am sure at least that you *can* have everything you want.'

'Everything?' he asked.

This was the moment. My moment. I smiled and said, 'Everything.'

The betrothal of Brochwel, prince of Dyfed, to an unknown young woman from a remote farming community, was announced the day after the feast. I had not left Brochwel's side since he beckoned me to join him at the castle gate. In a few short hours, we had become as one. My lover was captivated by me. He told me so, time and again, but even if his tongue had been cut out, I would have been able to read the devotion in his eyes. I felt intoxicated by the excitement of it all. For so long I had dreamed of a better life, and now it was coming true.

Yet soon several clouds emerged on the horizon. Pryderi was kind and attentive, but I suspected that not everyone was pleased by my arrival in the castle. In particular, I worried how Gowein, Brochwel's devoted mother, would regard me. Thus I took special pains to establish friendly relations with her. I told the story of my own mother's death and of how since childhood

I had missed the wise counsel of an older woman. When I said I prayed that she might supply the lack, she nodded gravely.

'You will be wife to my first born,' she said. 'I wish the two of you a long, happy and fruitful life together.'

Something in my expression must have given me away, for she clutched my hand and said earnestly, 'Fruitful, yes. Brochwel must have told you of our family's great sadness when both his children died in infancy.'

I nodded. Disease had carried off first the little boy and then his sister. Brochwel's wife had kept striving to give him an heir, but in the end she had died, agonisingly, in childbirth. The tragedy of her passing had deterred him from seeking an early remarriage, but he was keenly aware of the need to continue the line. I did not doubt his love for me, but I realised also that he saw in me a young, healthy woman, the ideal mother for a successor to his throne. I had no objection to that. I had always wanted to have children of my own, children of a man who adored me, children to whom I would recount legends in front of the fire, as my father had done to entertain Owain and me.

I cleared my throat. 'Gowein, there is something I wished to raise with you.'

She gripped my hand. 'What is it, my dear?'

'It is about Elfin.'

Yes, Elfin, brother to Brochwel.

Her face darkened. 'What about Elfin?'

'I do not believe…' My voice faltered. 'I am sorry, Gowein. It is nothing. Please forget that I mentioned his name.'

She squeezed my hand more tightly. 'Tell me, please.'

Her voice was clear and firm. Although she was no longer a young woman, she was accustomed to obedience and I found myself unable to refuse her instruction.

'I fear – I believe that he dislikes me.'

'What is it that makes you think that?' she demanded.

'Oh, I do not know. Perhaps I am imagining it. I am sure I have done nothing to cause him offence.'

'One does not need to provoke Elfin to earn his enmity,' Gowein said softly.

I was shocked by her words. She was his mother, after all. 'Forgive me,' I said hurriedly. 'It is just a fancy I have. He has not said anything unkind to me. At least, nothing deliberately unkind.'

'Even though...'

As Gowein began to speak, the door of the chamber swung open and a handsome dark-haired man appeared. He bore a resemblance to Brochwel in the shape of his cheeks and jaw, but the likeness seemed superficial. Where Brochwel was strong and commanding, this fellow was slender and almost womanish in the way he slipped into the room.

'I am sorry, mother. If I am interrupting....'

'Elfin,' Gowein said dryly. 'We were just talking about you.'

'Oh, really?' Amused, he shot a glance in my direction. 'Rhiannon, my dear. I shall soon have to learn to call you sister, won't I? Were you confessing to second thoughts? Telling mother that you weren't quite sure that you had chosen the right brother? I am much the younger man, of course. I do my brother no disservice by speaking plainly and saying that he is a man well past his prime.'

I curled my lip. In a short time, I had gained a confidence undreamed of during those long years spent toiling at the foot of the Preseli Hills.

'I promise you, Elfin, I have made no mistake.'

'Sure?' he prodded, a smirk upon his lips.

'Elfin!' his mother snapped. 'You are upgrown and yet you behave as badly as you did when you were a child. It will be the worse for you if Brochwel gets to hear that you have tormented Rhiannon.'

'I would sooner die than harm Rhiannon,' he said, affecting a noble pose.

'Elfin!' Gowein snapped. 'You have said enough.'

'But I only came here to express my congratulations,' he

said, pretending innocence. 'I have come from Brochwel's chamber. He tells me that the wedding is to take place on the last Saturday of this month. For him, the day cannot come soon enough. I tell you frankly, Rhiannon, my brother is besotted with you. It is as if you were a witch who has woven a spell upon him.'

'I am no witch,' I said, returning his gaze. 'I have but one object. I merely wish to make my husband happy.'

He gave me a frankly lascivious gaze and said, 'I am sure you will do just that.'

He turned and, at the door, paused. To his mother he said, 'Brochwel's tastes have always been simple to the point of crudity, have they not?'

When he was gone, I started to cry. Gowein came up to me and put an arm around my shoulder.

'Hush,' she said. 'You must take no notice of him. He was always a difficult boy. So unlike his brother. Where Brochwel was bluff and uncomplicated, Elfin always loved to scheme and make mischief. Perhaps it is my fault. He was born at a time when I thought I was past childbearing years. Brochwel was twenty and already hardened in combat. Perhaps that is why I spoiled Elfin. Besides, he has always possessed a certain charm.'

'I'm afraid it has escaped me,' I said, drying my tears.

'You must understand,' Gowein said. 'Elfin is jealous of his brother. He is intelligent and to him it seems unfair that he has no power. What he fails to realise is that he is no warrior, whereas Brochwel is fearless in battle. Elfin does not lack vanity, either. How often have I seen him preening when he thinks he is unobserved. In his way, he is a well-favoured man. But a pretty young thing like you was bound to choose a strong man ahead of a weakling.'

I shivered. 'He frightens me.'

'There is no need.' There was a note of decision in Gowein's voice. I guessed that she had made up her mind about something. 'I shall speak to Brochwel this very evening. He will despatch Elfin on business in Ireland where he can do no harm.'

I was struck, then and always, by Gowein's lack of sentimentality. Elfin was her flesh and blood, no less than Brochwel, but she could look without flinching into his heart. She was determined, too, and although at first Brochwel was reluctant to send his brother across the sea, eventually he assented. I spoke to him that night about the matter and mentioned my dislike of Elfin.

'Ah, he is not as bad as you suggest,' Brochwel said.

'I believe he is much worse.'

Brochwel laughed. He was in high good humour and proved it by pushing his hand beneath my dress. I shrieked and tried in vain to dance out of his reach. Within a few moments, my apprehensions were forgotten.

Elfin did not return to Dyfed in time to attend the wedding. I was not sorry. I wanted nothing to distract me on that special day. Owain and Keneldon did make the journey, and it struck me as a delicious irony that after my long years of innocence I had married before even they had taken their vows.

And what a marriage I had made! My husband looked every inch the prince he was. He towered over his people in every sense. He towered over me – except when the two of us were alone and I could make him do my bidding, have him kneel and plead for my good word.

The showers of spring gave way to the burning sun of summer, the hottest I could recall. Shortly after our wedding, I discovered that I was with child. Gowein, as a woman would, guessed the truth, but before I was ready to give the news to my husband, I lost the baby. My indisposition caused me to be confined to a room of my own on the ground floor of the castle, but both Brochwel and his mother were equally solicitous. One morning he admitted to me that Gowein had told him what had happened.

'You will have another baby,' he announced.

I smiled. 'As it happens, I felt better on waking than I have done since – since it happened.'

'You are ready to return to the marriage bed?'

He was breathing heavily. I knew how impatient my husband was for an heir. The long years of battle had taken their toll. He had resolved to live each day as if it were his last.

'Tonight,' I nodded.

He beamed and his happiness was so infectious that I smiled as I said, 'I have missed you, Brochwel.'

'At last we can be man and wife again,' he said eagerly, enfolding me in his bear-like embrace.

'You have been so patient,' I said as soon as I managed to recover my breath.

'It has not been easy,' he confessed.

'Then perhaps you deserve a reward.'

He smiled at me, wondering what I had in mind. When I told him, he let out an exuberant shout of delight.

I had promised to give my husband his prize at a place which held special memories for us. On the afternoon following the feast, he had taken me to the coast and we had made love on the shore of a lonely cove. I took him back there and we walked hand in hand along the beach, teasing each other about names we might give to our child. It would, of course, be a boy.

Brochwel pulled me down on to the sand and started to undress, but I jumped up again and skipped out of reach. When he lumbered after me, I raised a hand and told him to shut his eyes and count to one hundred.

'What do you have in mind?' He was sweating in the heat. I could smell his excitement.

'Trust me.'

He closed his eyes as instructed and I ran off, laughing as I scrambled up the steep slopes of the cliff. I could hear him counting, slowly, carefully.

'Seventeen, eighteen, nineteen.'

The way up the cliff was narrow and difficult. I suppose it was dangerous, but that did not concern me. My father and Owain had nicknamed me The Sheep, because of my sure-footed climbing skills. This was no more of a challenge than the Freni Fawr at the eastern end of the Preseli mountains.

'Sixty-nine, seventy, seventy-one.'

Panting, I pulled myself up on to the summit. Once I was on firm ground, I began to tear off my clothes with reckless abandon. Brochwel's voice was distant now, drifting up in the light summer breeze.

'Ninety-two, ninety-three, ninety-four.'

Naked, I peered down to sea level and my husband. The drop was almost sheer, but it did not frighten me.

'Come to claim your reward!' I cried as he reached one hundred.

He opened his eyes and looked up at me. I smiled and waved. With a cry of pleasure, he began to clamber up the cliff. Not for one moment did I doubt that he would reach the peak. Although he was heavily built, he too was accustomed to rough terrain. I heard him panting as he hurried up towards me. I moved back from the precipice and lay down on the parched grass, waiting for Brochwel to claim me.

We made love with a passion I had never known with him before, and when we were done, I demanded more. He gave a roar of ecstasy and complied, but even as he entered me again, he let out a different kind of cry, a cry of pain and dismay.

'What is it?' I gasped.

Suddenly he pitched over and collapsed on to his side, clutching his heart.

'Brochwel?' I cried. 'Brochwel?'

*

A week after the funeral, I was sitting alone in my chamber, as had become my custom since Brochwel's death. Elfin had returned to the castle as soon as he heard the news and taken charge. He was now the Prince of Dyfed and I no more than a weeping widow. Small wonder that I stayed in my room, staring out of the little window at the moon which shone above the sleeping town, trying to conjure a picture in my mind of what the future might hold.

Gowein had told Elfin that he must show me kindness. He had assented readily enough. He was in command now and could afford to be generous. I saw little of him, as he took pains to respect my mourning, but in his mother's presence he told me that I was, naturally, welcome to treat the castle as my home. He said he was determined that, in time, he and I should become the best of friends.

It was beyond doubt that Gowein was affected even more than I was by the death of her son. For all her strength, she was looking old and defeated. If Brochwel's heart had burst, hers had surely broken. I tried once or twice to engage her in conversation, but she did no more than indulge in a few banal pleasantries before saying that her head ached and that she needed rest.

Suddenly I heard a dreadful scream. My imagination playing tricks? Surely there could be no other explanation. I pulled my wrap around me and opened the door. I expected darkness, but instead I saw the faint flicker of a candle, hovering above the passageway. Chilled to the bone, I stopped in my tracks. In the dead of night, I could not help remembering my father's stories and his tale of the Corpse Candle.

How absurd. Even as I waited, the flame disappeared. I must have dreamed it, as well as the scream. I took a step forward, then paused again. I could hear footsteps coming in my direction. Holding my breath, I saw another flame lighting up the gloom, moving closer to me.

'Who is it?' I called out.

'It is me, Gowein.'

My mother-in-law sounded strangely agitated. I waited as she approached.

'What are you doing abroad at this hour?' I asked.

Her face appeared, illumined by the flame. 'Did you hear the scream?'

'I wondered – if I had been having a nightmare.'

'You did not imagine that scream,' she said, reaching out and taking my hand.

Her touch was cold and I recoiled from it, but her grip tightened. 'Gowein,' I stammered. 'I do not understand. What is happening?'

'You are afraid?'

'Yes.'

'Afraid – of Elfin?'

'Of Elfin?' I repeated stupidly. 'What do you mean?'

'I have always been afraid of Elfin,' she said. 'Ever since he was a small boy, tearing the wings off flies.'

'Since his return he has been good to me,' I said.

'Oh yes, now that he has what he always wanted.' She gave a bitter laugh and led me into my room. 'Come. I shall tell you about Elfin.'

We sat down side by side on the edge of my rumpled bed. 'Gowein,' I said gently, for I had begun to suspect that the loss of her elder son had pushed her into madness. 'You are talking in riddles. What is this about Elfin?'

'He was jealous of Brochwel,' she said. 'Even as a child, he envied his brother. I saw it, but I was too weak. There was an incident with an axe – passed off as horseplay, but Brochwel came within inches of losing his head.'

'You cannot be saying that Elfin wanted Brochwel dead? I do not believe it!'

'It is true,' Gowein insisted. 'Later, while Brochwel travelled far and wide, Elfin retreated within himself. He was such a good-looking boy that I was ready to forgive and forget.

Forgive his wickedness, forget the harm that he wanted to do to his brother. Stupid of me.'

'Elfin is not violent!' I cried. 'He is bookish, not in the least a warrior.'

'Nonetheless, I hold him responsible for Brochwel's death.'

'What are you talking about? I cried, genuinely alarmed. 'That was a tragic accident.'

'I think not,' Gowein said. 'I believe my son was murdered, as truly as if Elfin had plunged a dagger into his heart.'

'This is madness!' I sobbed. 'You do not know what you are saying.'

She gazed into my eyes. 'I am afraid I know precisely what I am saying, Rhiannon. As you do.'

'You accuse me?' I gasped.

'Something puzzled me,' Gowein said in a faraway voice. 'I believed that you and Elfin had schemed to kill Brochwel, but I did not understand how the conspiracy could have originated. Stray words from my late sister's boy, Pryderi, confirmed my suspicions of Elfin. I asked Pryderi to undertake a little detective work on my behalf and he reported back this evening. I gather that you visited St David's at the same time as Elfin was there. That was where you met. I suppose the pair of you fell in love. At least, I hope it was love. At all events, you hatched your plot. You would travel to Pembroke with a view to seducing Brochwel and becoming his bride.'

'Absurd!'

'No false modesty, Rhiannon, please. For such a beauty, it was not a difficult task. The first part of your plan accomplished, you had a further goal. Elfin confided in you that Brochwel's heart was frail, a secret known only to the three of us. Elfin wanted you to contrive the circumstances where his brother's heart would be strained to bursting point. Then you could safely leave nature to take its course.' She paused. 'As it did when you lost Brochwel's child. Or are my darker suspicions founded in truth? Did you give nature a helping hand so that you did not give birth to a baby sired by a husband for whom you cared nothing?'

'This is intolerable!'

'I agree,' Gowein said. 'Alas, it is also true.'

'You believe I betrayed my husband and connived to ensure his death? You dare to suggest that I destroyed my own unborn child out of sheer malice?'

'Acts of such wickedness,' she said softly, 'cannot go unpunished.'

'I suppose,' I murmured, 'you claim that we wanted Elfin to be sent far away so that no one could hint that he played a part in Brochwel's death?'

'You acted so prettily,' Gowein said. 'I genuinely believed that you disliked Elfin. Instead, you lusted after him.'

'I came to realise,' I said slowly, 'that much of what you said about him was true.'

'You were his dupe,' she said, not troubling to hide her scorn.

'He is your own flesh and blood – and yet you hate him.'

'For his cruelty. Even a mother cannot remain blind forever.' Gowein shrugged. 'But he will do no more harm.'

'What do you mean?'

For answer, she reached inside her gown and pulled out a knife. Touching the blade, I felt a warm stickiness upon it.

'I have killed my own son,' she said in a hollow voice.

'And now you intend to kill me.' I gave a bitter laugh. 'I should have realised when I saw the Corpse Candle.'

There was a look of sorrow in her eyes. 'There is nothing else I can do. Brochwel must be avenged.'

She lifted the knife, but I was younger and faster and more desperate. I seized her wrist and forced it downwards. I heard the bone snap and then the blade plunged into her breast. She cried out and slipped backwards. I forced the knife home and within a moment I was standing over her body. Yes, the Corpse Candle had presaged another death. But not mine.

I heard footsteps in the darkness.

'They are all gone!' I cried. 'Brochwel, Elfin, Gowein.'

And Pryderi, my handsome Pryderi, came running down the corridor, running into my arms.

Nine months have passed since then, my little one. Pryderi, the same Pryderi with whom I fell in love when he gave me Brochwel's message, is the Prince of Dyfed and I am his proud consort. Tonight our union has been given a special blessing. I have presented him with a son and heir.

Your birth was slow and agonising, my sweet. There was a time when I believed that neither of us would survive. But now you are here in my arms, a small warm bundle of humanity. I have a child of my own, a child to love and cherish, a child to whom I shall tell stories of wizards and saints and fearsome beasts. Yet I shall make no further mention of the Corpse Candle. There will be no more deaths in this household. For you and I shall live happily ever after.

Margaret Murphy

A CERTAIN RESOLUTION

He watched from the warmth of his car. She was home. The curtains were drawn, but the lights glowed behind them and he tracked her movement around the house as one set of lights went off and another went on. He felt a confused mixture of desire and anger. When she had first rejected him, he hung around her flat, hurt, hoping that she would take him back. For days – *weeks* – he played Heathcliffe to her Cathy. When she became irritated by his persistence, he was embittered: wasn't he trying to protect her, to keep her safe?

He couldn't say exactly when he began to enjoy the vigil; the feeling grew slowly, and it was bound up with the change in her attitude, from impatience to anxiety. He had provoked it, he knew, with a telephone warning or two, a letter telling her just how much she needed him, but once it began, her fear seemed to feed on itself, and he became hungry for it. He no longer wanted her to take him back – her fear convinced him that he could take what he wanted whenever he liked. What thrilled and sustained him during the long nights of watching was the look of terror on her face when she saw his car parked outside her flat, the tremor in her voice when she answered the phone.

The night he broke into her flat was the most perfect sex he had ever had. Her response to his rage proved a potent aphrodisiac. But he hadn't frightened her enough, it seemed, because the next day the police had come for him.

Prison had changed him: he had lost some of his easy self-confidence, his persuasive charm. It had been replaced by

137

something much harder, and more dangerous. He had nothing but Emma now. He had lost his job and the Mondeo that went with it, his flat had been re-let, and he found his friends no longer keen for his company: it seemed they feared for their potato-faced wives.

Emma was the root cause of all his present problems, and yet he still wanted her. And he wanted Emma to think about him every waking minute of her day. He wanted to preoccupy her thoughts, her dreams, her nightmares. He would dictate the detail of her plans, whether it was making a decision about taking a job, or something as simple as making a trip to the shops.

Orange light from the street lamps reflected in the puddles from the most recent downpour, but the sky was clearing, and the moon shone cold and austere on the slate roofs of the terraced houses. It was seven o'clock, and families were settling down for the night. The street was a cul-de-sac, so the residents provided the only traffic, and it seemed no one was keen to go out on this cold November night.

He planned to wait until the last light went out in the house, then watch for the glow of her bedside lamp. Emma no longer slept in the dark; that was down to him, and he thought of it as a bond between them. She slept at the front of the house, perhaps thinking that she would be able to raise the alarm more easily from there, but when he got to her, he wouldn't allow so much as a squeak from her.

He was about to close his eyes and snooze for a short while when he saw a light go on in the hallway and Emma's front door opened. This was the first time he had seen her since the courtroom when she had given her evidence. She looked thinner – he was always telling her she should lose some weight, and now, finally, she had. A dog bounced around at her feet, a German Shepherd. He evaluated it and judged it to be no more than a puppy, floppy-eared and lolloping. It posed no threat.

138

When Emma turned and closed the door, he saw with a shock that she had cut her hair; her beautiful long hair chopped to collar length.

Christ! She looks like a bloody dyke!

She locked the door – a Yale deadlock and a heavy-looking mortise – and looked anxiously up and down the street before crossing within ten feet of his car. He slid down in his seat, then swivelled to see where she was going.

She walked with her head down, as if willing herself invisible, her soft-soled shoes barely making a sound on the pavement. She was heading for an area of fenced woodland that started at the end of the road and circled around one side of the estate, though not, he noted, the back of Emma's house. What was she trying to prove, going out on her own in the dark? This was just the sort of behaviour that got her into trouble the first time around.

She opened a narrow wooden gate and let the dog through, only allowing it off the leash when she was on the other side herself. He *could* leave her to it: wait for her to get back, and then carry on as he had planned. There again, he could let himself into her house and wait for her. Or he could go after her. Maybe he would, just for a bit – kick up a few leaves, make a bit of noise – remind her why a woman shouldn't go out alone at night. Show her how much use her 'guard' dog really was.

He grabbed his rucksack from the well of the passenger seat. It contained everything he needed: syringe, morphine, knife, rope, gag, condoms – he wasn't going to get caught the same way twice.

He walked incautiously, snapping twigs, scuffing up the sodden mulch of autumnal litter. Once or twice he thought he heard an answering *crack!*, a rustling in the undergrowth. He kept an eye out for the dog: if it doubled back to investigate him, he might need the knife.

The path twisted and veered right down between two mounds; bare except for a few strippy saplings, they resembled giant anthills. Here the leaf litter from the overhanging beech and oak trees was thickly layered and, wet with rainfall, it deadened every sound.

She whistled.

He stood perfectly still, watching to see where the dog emerged from. It gave a bark, as if it had found something in the undergrowth, but Emma whistled again and called its name, and it came running, its tongue lolling and ears flapping.

She hadn't seen him. She patted the dog and turned the bend, descending into a cut behind one of the hillocks.

He followed at a trot, the moonlight bright enough for him to negotiate safely the ruts and dips in the path down into the cut. The wind boomed through the upper branches of the trees. It was darker here, and colder. He walked on, more cautiously now, rounded a bend, and stopped dead, disconcerted by what he saw.

Emma stood, her hands by her sides, no more than ten or fifteen feet away. Her face shone as grey as the moon. There was no sign of the pup, but he heard a whimper and a tentative bark from somewhere behind her.

For a while – it seemed a long time, but it couldn't have been more than half a minute – they did nothing. This wasn't how it was supposed to happen. *He* was supposed to choose the time and place. He had waited long enough, thought about it, planned every detail. There was little else to do in prison; he had refined and rehearsed and perfected every stage of his 'new vigil' as he thought of it, and now she had messed it all up.

Well, he thought, shucking the rucksack from his shoulder. *She asked for it.*

Suddenly Emma was moving. She walked towards him; quick, purposeful strides, her head down, avoiding his eyes. He had taught her never to give him that brazen look, and he was gratified that she hadn't forgotten the lesson.

She's going to ask me to leave her alone. She's going to beg.

'Oh, you'll beg, all right,' he murmured, squeezing the clip on the front flap of his bag.

The dog barked, another anxious yelp. He thought he saw a shadow flit from one tree to the next at the periphery of his vision. Emma might not be the only dog-walker dragging their pet out for a toilet break between the rain showers – he would have to be quick. He reached into his rucksack, felt the hilt of the knife.

Then she was on him.

A flash of cold light – the glint of a blade.

He pulled, feeling a rising panic. His knife snagged on the material of the flap. Too late. *Too late!*

He lifted the rucksack, using it as a shield.

She drove forward, tearing through the nylon bag, through the padding of his jacket, barely making contact with his flesh. He felt a popping sensation, a sharp shock. He dropped the rucksack and covered his stomach with his hands.

She pulled back, came at him again. In the slow, choreographed moments that followed, he saw that the blade was dulled with blood – his blood. He looked into her face and saw nothing. No fear, no hatred. No emotion at all. He made a grab for her hand and caught the knife blade instead. It sliced his flesh with a faint wet hiss and he felt a vivid burning pain in his hand.

Emma plunged the knife inwards and upwards.

John Baker

DEFENCE

1

Father's Volvo was parked on the quay as we drew into Bekkelagskaia. From the ship's rail I could make out his silhouette slowly growing larger as we approached. He had left the car and was shading his eyes against the sun, looking towards the ship. I had nothing to say to him. I had changed my mind about returning to Norway almost as soon as the ship set sail. One should never go back, I told myself. And yet for me there didn't seem to be a way forward. I wanted Hazel, my wife, and Tor, my son, and they were in the past. I couldn't go back to them. I could never go back.

Father came up the ship's gangplank and shook me by the hand. 'Trond,' he said.

'Far,' I said. There was a smile on his face and disappointment in his eyes.

'Velkommen.'

'Thanks.' His eyes held me for a moment and swung me back into the merry-go-round of childhood and adolescence. The language, though coming instinctively to my tongue, seemed to change my centre of balance. An uncomfortable feeling, like the removing of several layers of skin. I wrenched myself free and looked out over the water to the islands. 'It's beautiful,' I said.

He followed my gaze towards Malmoya and Ulvoya. 'Yes,' he said. 'We have a beautiful country.' It was certainly different to the murky, smog laden Humber which had been my point of departure from England. The physical beauty was a welcome sight.

We spoke little on the drive into Oslo, and I was thankful for my father's tact, not least because I knew he was bursting with questions. But I needed a breathing space, and he could see that. He was calm on the surface, controlled; we were both calm and controlled.

My mother came out of the house and took my bag. She placed a dry kiss on my cheek and stood back with the same disappointed eyes as my father. The disappointment was genuine: I was their son and I had failed. But it also masked a triumph, for I had returned to them and to their beloved country, and they had always known I would. Not now, but later they would tell me so.

We drank coffee and talked about my journey. They spoke of cousins and old school friends, of the New Norwegian Theatre, and Scandinavian politics. Hazel and Tor were not mentioned, my marriage, my life in England were all avoided as taboo subjects. They were all there, larger than life in the midst of us, but heavily veiled. They would be brought out in the evening, after dinner, when my brother and sister would also be there. I would have to talk about it, confess, answer their questions. But it would be better later than now. There was a kind of safety in numbers.

I spent the afternoon in my room. My old room. The room in which I had spent my childhood. It had nothing to do with me. There were many things still there, things I had left behind years before. But there was nothing I wanted. Books I had never read, toys I no longer recognised. My mother would never throw them out. They reminded her of her little boy, her life as a young woman and mother. They reminded her of her dreams.

I wept on the bed. Weeping had become a habit. I no longer screamed with the pain, the injustice, the incomprehension. I

143

wept quietly, alone. The weeping was a kind of comfort now, though often it was difficult to stop. I had little control over it. It was easy to start and not easy to stop. I wallowed in self-pity, in self-justification. It seemed all right to do that. It harmed no one, and I hoped that eventually my tears would dry up, that my soul would not be too damaged by the damming up of my feelings.

The events of that day, the day of my arrival in Norway are burned into my memory. I have puzzled long over why that should be so, but I am still not really clear. Perhaps it is because returning to Norway was the first positive thing I did since Hazel told me the one thing I was not capable of hearing. I was welcome in Norway, of that I had no doubt. What I doubted was whether I wanted to be welcome in that way. What my parents, my brother and sister, and friends welcomed was not the me I had become during my time in England, but something I had ceased to be. The Trond I had been in their imagination many years before, the child and adolescent who was experienced only in innocence.

I imagined at that time that I would spend only a few weeks in Norway, perhaps a month or two, before returning to England. But I was there nineteen months before the telephone call came, and I might have stayed for ever, tidily wrapped in the trivia of my flag-waving family, if it had not been for that one event.

The dining table was set with candles. Mother and father sat at the head and foot of the table. The rest of us were placed at my mother's discretion. I to her right, with my sister, Siv, between me and father. My brother, Jon, sat opposite me, and my sister's husband, Ola, was next to him. We ate crayfish with Retsina, a ritual dish in the family, used only for special occasions. Father kept our glasses filled with the Retsina, and we each made a border on our plates with the heads of the crayfish.

My diplomatic father asked Ola and Siv about their children, and there followed several anecdotes about the absent generation. Then Siv turned to me.

'And what about Tor?' she asked.

'He's well,' I said trying to keep any trace of emotion from my voice. 'He's not walking yet, but I don't think it'll be long.'

'And Hazel?' The table had become so quiet that I could hear their breathing. I swallowed and clutched at the napkin on my lap.

'She's OK,' I said. 'They're both OK.' I wanted to go on, to keep talking, to maintain the initiative with myself, but at the mention of Hazel's name my mouth dried up. It was all too close to me, the family's expectations too pressing. I stopped talking and looked down at my plate, adjusting one of the crays' heads, putting it in line with the others.

Silence hung over us for a few moments, and then Siv drew in her breath. 'You don't have to go into details,' she said. 'But you'll have to tell us something.'

'We've split up,' I said quietly. 'We no longer live together.'

'Yes,' said Siv. 'And Tor is with Hazel?'

'They're still in York, in the same house. I moved out two months ago.'

'Two months!' Siv was right to be surprised, I had only contacted them the week before I sailed.

'I didn't say anything about it before. I thought there might be a chance of us getting back together.'

'It's permanent, then?'

I nodded.

Mother moved her hand towards mine, but stopped short before she reached me. Our hands lay side by side on the table.

'Is there someone else?' asked Siv.

'No,' I said. I couldn't tell them about him. I couldn't even bear to think about him.

'But why, then, Trond?' asked my mother, echoing the question I had asked myself a million times. 'We thought you were so happy, so suited.'

'Hazel needed to live by herself,' I lied. 'It wasn't her fault. We come from different cultures, we have different expectations. It just didn't work.'

'But it worked for two years,' said my father.

'And then it didn't work any longer.'

'And Tor?' he said. 'Will we see him again?'

'Yes. Maybe not for a while. But when he's older I'll have him for holidays.'

My mother breathed a sigh of relief. She wouldn't have been able to cope with her grandson never seeing Norway and not learning to speak the language.

'And there's no hope for you and Hazel?' asked Siv.

'No.' I shook my head. 'I don't think so.'

They accepted it eventually. They all of them accepted it much more than I did. It had always been unacceptable to me, and I knew that it always would be. But as the months passed it became more bearable. I learned new techniques for dealing with it, kept it close to myself. Whenever the subject of marriage came up I sidestepped it, spoke in generalities and struggled to stop myself drowning in the turbulent sea of images of Hazel, my wife, Tor, my son; and the other one, the image of him who had destroyed it all.

Hazel and I exchanged irregular and pragmatic letters, and after eleven months in Norway I spent a few days in York to see Tor. Hazel invited me to the house, but I didn't want to see *him*, so arranged for her to bring Tor to my hotel. He was twenty months old, and after clinging to his mother he tottered around the furniture quite independently. He was dark, with Hazel's hair, but a distinctive Norwegian nose. He didn't know me and wouldn't sit on my knee, but before they left he let me hold his hand, and I ruffled his hair and managed to plant a wet kiss on his forehead. They stayed for two hours. Hazel was very pregnant.

I resolved to see him regularly after that, though the experience of meeting him and Hazel together had almost destroyed me. I would have to move back to England to be closer to my son. I couldn't bear him growing up and not knowing who I was.

But it didn't happen. I stayed on in Norway. I know now that I was waiting for that telephone call, but I didn't know it then. For the next eight months my destiny was adjourned. All the time I was intending to return to England, but the forces of my will never came together enough for me to make the step.

Before breakfast on the seventh of January that year the telephone rang.

'Trond?'

It was *his* voice. My impulse was to put the telephone down. I felt the beginnings of rage stir inside me.

'Trond?' he said again. 'Don't put the phone down. Just listen to me. Hazel's dead. There's been an accident.'

He was silent. I couldn't think of anything to say. The rage disseminated and mingled with incomprehension and disbelief.

'Trond? Are you there?'

'Yes,' I said. 'How? When?'

'She was in the car. She hit a bus.'

'Tor?'

'He's all right. He was with me. Both of the kids were with me.'

'I want him back,' I said.

There was a long silence. Then he said, 'We'll have to talk about it. Will you come here?'

'Yes,' I said. 'And I want Tor back.'

'Let me know when you'll arrive,' he said. 'The funeral will be on Monday, the thirteenth.'

I put the telephone down and sank to my knees on the floor, my head in my hands. I expected to weep, to scream, anything. But nothing happened. I don't know how long I stayed there, anaesthetised within a dull cocoon of dark silence, before I stood and walked out of the house, ready at last to pick up the remains of my shattered destiny.

2

I had lived in dread of seeing him, even of hearing his voice. Anything that reminded me of him was enough to throw me into a rage. If I read a book or newspaper and came across his name, I would stop reading. There was violence in me, a dark and overwhelmingly powerful force; a volcano that slumbered uneasily beneath the gentle contours of social manners, but that could erupt without warning into an inferno of destruction. I knew it was there, and that he could unwittingly be the agent of its release.

The voice on the telephone had not affected me in this way, because the message it brought had swamped those baser instincts and feelings. It left me only with the picture of Hazel crushed in the wreckage of her car. Gentle, stupid Hazel, who had destroyed me, and who had now destroyed herself. The picture was a moving image, like a clip from a film. There was a close-up of Hazel, head and shoulders at the wheel, a slight smile on her lips as she glanced into the mirror. Her eyes were bright and quick, like the eyes of a wild animal, and they held no presentiment of fear, saw nothing of what was to come.

The camera panned back and away to the right, and the images faltered into slow motion as the car concertinaed into the oncoming bus, the rear wheels lifting themselves clear of the ground and the nose burrowing deeper into itself. Her dark head shattered through the windscreen, sending a shower of crystals high into the air. And then, still in slow motion, the camera closed in on the body, wantonly recording the helpless, ragged shaking as it was flung from side to side over the crippled bonnet of the car, the legs still pinned under the strangled steering column.

Then there was stillness. Silence.
The picture slowly faded, leaving a shining white screen.
Slut.

After the telephone call I walked. Hazel was dead, laid out somewhere on a slab, maybe in a deep freeze. She would never answer my questions now, never come back. I walked and talked with her in my head, seeing her as she had been on all the other occasions: at our wedding; the long holiday in Norway with crossed skis; cradling Tor in her arms the day after he was born. The adultress was there too, in her furious love for him and her unreasonable hatred of me. But I could not hear what she said, only the incessant whining of my own pain, the chattering rant of my disbelief. And superimposed on all these flickering images was the one Hazel I had not yet met: the dead one.

I walked along Kirkeveien and stood dwarfed in the snow beneath Vigeland's grotesque human monolith. Hazel was dead and I walked. The Buddha was right to recognise the fact of suffering. It is the only reality. He was wrong about everything else.

I took a short cut through the Slottsparken, past the National Theatre, and along Karl Johans Gate. It was snowing hard, very cold, and my chin and feet were numb. I had not eaten, simply fled the house and the black telephone. I sat under Per Krohg's huge painting of the Christianian Bohemians in the Grand Café and watched their affluent descendants stuffing themselves from the smorgasbord.

The coffee was black and bitter, scalding hot, putting the illusion of strength back into my body. Strength which I wanted to conserve, but which I knew I would squander. I was ready to leave, to walk aimlessly round the city, when a child at the next table reminded me. I had a son. Tor, my English son. He would soon be three years old.

I had quoted Novalis to Hazel on the day he was born:

Children are hopes. The nurse held him up to the glass and pulled away the shawl from his face. We were not allowed to meet.

A year later I had returned to Norway, leaving him with his mother. The bond between us, stretched to its limit, was torn apart. After that we had spent two hours together in a York hotel. Before he left he let me hold his hand, and I ruffled his hair and managed to plant a wet kiss on his forehead.

And that was all there was between me and my son. Except that during our first year together he had become more important to me than food. In his absence I had hungered for him, sometimes literally clawing at my belly, my mouth and throat dry with longing. My soul had grown thin and emaciated without him, and whenever I formed his image, so small, so young, so far away, I felt the rhythm of my heart stumble with fear for him.

He needed me, of that I had no doubt. A boy needs a father. No one would ever love him as unselfishly, as impossibly as I did. I loved him totally, as a cow loves grass. And he didn't want me to go. If he had had words he would have argued with Hazel more forcibly than I could. During the long discussions with Hazel before I left, the mention of Tor was taboo. Whatever I said about him was emotional blackmail.

Her mind was made up. She had convinced herself that Tor, as well as herself, would be better off without me. By that time she had built up a protective wall around herself. She no longer listened to my ravings, she was beyond my reach. She could only be touched by him.

Later I went to the telephone and dialled the numbers. He answered almost immediately, as if he had been sat by the phone waiting for it to ring. His voice was quiet, subdued, but insistent.

'Hello. Hello. Who is it?' He repeated the number I had dialled.

'It's Trond,' I said.

'Trond? Oh, yes.'

'Listen. I've made some arrangements.' I kept the index finger of my right hand on the notes I had made.

'Are you coming?'

'Yes. I've booked a flight for tonight. I'll stay in the same hotel as before.'

'You can stay here if you like.'

'No. I'll stay in the hotel.'

'What about Tor?'

He was getting ahead of my notes. I had to stay in command of the conversation. 'Can you listen to what I have to say. I'm trying to make arrangements.'

'Sorry. Go on.'

'I'll stay in the same hotel as before. I don't want you to come and see me there, or even to contact me, unless there is an emergency. Do you understand?'

'Yes, but…'

'Good. Next, I want you to give me the name of the hospital and exact address so I can see Hazel.'

'We're moving her out of the hospital. She's going to a private funeral parlour.' He gave me the address and I read it back to him.

'The date and time of the funeral?'

'It's not fixed exactly. I'll have to tell you later.'

'No. You can tell Hazel's parents. I'll find out from them. Leave Tor there, together with all his clothes and toys, and I'll collect him.'

'What do you mean?'

'I'll collect him from his grandparents.'

'And?'

'And what? He'll come back to Norway with me.'

There was a long silence. I thought he had rung off.

'Hello,' I said.

'Yes. I'm still here. Are you serious?'

151

'Yes. He's my son. You have no jurisdiction over him.'

'Maybe not, but he doesn't know you. He doesn't know what's happening. You can't just drag him away to a foreign country.'

'I want him back.'

'Maybe you do, Trond. But it'll have to be a slow process. He's part of a family here, you can't destroy all his roots.'

'You can't keep him. He's my son.'

'But think about it from his point of view. If you really want him back I won't interfere, but you'd have to give him time to get to know you. He's crying for his mother at the moment.'

I could see that: Tor, my son, crying for his mother. It was a vivid picture. Part of me rushed away across the sea towards him, leaving a ghost holding the telephone in Oslo. My notes fluttered to the floor, and my mouth dried out, cracking my voice.

'Look after him,' I said helplessly.

There was a short silence.

'Sure,' he said. 'Don't worry, he'll be all right. Come and see us when you get here. We can talk and decide what to do for the best. It would be all right for you to stay here.'

'No,' I said. 'I couldn't do that.'

'Are you sure?'

'Yes.'

'But you'll come and see us?'

I nodded my head.

'Yes,' I croaked. 'Yes. I'll come.'

3

The door opened and we stood facing each other. He smiled tiredly. He was frailer than I remembered, his pale face contrasted with the dark passage behind him, and for a moment I was out of my body and viewing our meeting from somewhere above. The ghost-like figure of him on the inside of the door, and the bulky otherness of me standing opposite him.

'Come in,' he said. His smile, finding no reflection in me, withered away. I followed him into one of the rooms at the back of the house, aware that I was acting a part, conscious that I was unprepared for the role, but that, in the circumstances, I was making a good job of it.

I loosened the buttons of my coat, a prickly sweat breaking over my neck and forehead. There was a smell of urine which became more prominent as we entered the room. Tor, aware of my alien presence, quickly picked up the toy cars he was driving along the carpet, and hid himself behind the man's legs. The baby girl, left alone on the carpet, half shuffled, half crawled towards the sanctuary of her father. I tried not to take their flight personally.

He went down on his knees, enclosing each of the children with an arm, holding them close to his body. 'It's all right,' he told them softly. 'We've got a visitor. Tor's daddy has come to see us.'

They looked up at me, the tall giant, the all-powerful stranger from another world. I smiled down on them, stupidly, the bitter-sweet ammonia stinging my nostrils and clinging freely to my skin. I couldn't visualise the image I presented to them: Tor's daddy, Odin, the great father.

'We'll make a drink, shall we,' said the man, standing. 'Will you have tea?' he asked.

'Yes, please.'

'And some juice for Tor and Christine.'

I followed them into the kitchen. 'Shall I take your coat?' he said. He took it to a hanger in the hall, unconsciously stealing the power. Odin, the Sun-being, was obscured by the clouds of routine. I was a visitor in an English home. Their home. The awe of their first scrutiny was superseded by the expectation of lemonade.

'Good trip?' he asked.

'Yes, it was all right.'

He lifted Christine and strapped her into a high chair. Tor scrambled on to another chair next to her, and they were served with red juice in plastic cups with lids.

'Have you seen the body?' he asked, setting a teapot and two cups on the table.

'No. I was going after lunch.'

'You've got the address?'

'Yes. I know where it is.'

'Good,' he said. 'Christine, don't pour it all over the table. It's for drinking.' He took the cup from her and returned it the right way up.

'Do you like juice?' I asked Tor. He ignored me. 'You look as though you do.' He put his plastic cup on the table and pushed it away.

'Oh, I'll drink it, then,' said the man, reaching out for the cup.

'No.' Tor took it back quickly, holding it close to his chest.

'Tor, do you remember Trond?' said the man. But the child wouldn't be drawn. Not only did he not remember, he refused to acknowledge my existence.

'Can I have a drink of your juice?' I tried. There was no response. Christine sprinkled the table again, and her father mopped it up with a dishcloth.

'More tea?' he asked. But I hadn't yet started to drink the first cup.

'I would have liked to talk,' I said.

'Yes, it's not really possible during the day. You could come back this evening.'

'Yes. About eight?'

'OK,' he said. Hazel's expression. Everything was OK to her. 'The offer of a room is still open if you change your mind. Tor and Christine would like that, wouldn't you?'

Tor and Christine didn't seem too taken with the idea. I shook my head.

'The house is bloody empty these last days,' he said, almost to himself. 'Since, ever since…' There was a perceptible crack in his voice, and I feared he would break down. Christine started banging the table with her cup, and Tor joined in, an almost rhythmic drumming, ancient, as if to resurrect some mysterious power from the beginnings of the world. They gradually increased the pace, rising to a crescendo which promised chaos. The man sat with his head in his hands, his will given up to some inner necessity, and I realised instinctively that if order was to be resumed, it was up to me to do something about it.

The drumming was insistent, like the insatiable rant of war.

'Shhhhhhhh,' I said gently, introducing breath into the situation, as one would introduce rain to a fire. 'Shhhhhhhh.' Tor stopped immediately, his cup poised in mid-air, caught in its downward journey. Christine continued drumming for a few more strokes, but with less force, and at my third 'Hushhhhh' she stopped completely.

'You'll give him a headache,' I said, indicating their father, who was emerging from his hands.

'I'm sorry,' he said. 'I'm overtired.'

'He's too tired,' said Tor.

'I haven't slept much,' he explained. 'There's so much to do. If someone else was here it would be better.'

I hesitated. Tor had spoken to me. I turned to him and said, 'What about you, Tor? Are you too tired?' He ignored me again. 'Could I help?' I asked the man.

He said nothing, only looked at me through vacant grey eyes.

'All right,' I said. 'I'll stay for a few days.'

I slept during the afternoon, before checking out of the hotel and taking a taxi to Charles's house. I could start to think of him as Charles now, after years of denying him a name, of begrudging his existence. I had no love for him, did not like him, but he no longer stood between me and Hazel, was no longer a threat.

155

He was ill. His eyes blazed with fire. He showed me the room I would use, told me to help myself to anything, then crept off to his own room, a tartan blanket wrapped round his shoulders, his whole body shaking with fever.

I explored the house. The house that had been my house, our house. The house from which I had been banished. It had not altered, the furniture was basically the same, the pictures on the walls, even the books on the shelves. Some of the carpets had been replaced, the walls painted, the curtains washed. The signature to everything was Hazel's.

I made the tea on a tray and took it to Charles's room, tapping lightly on the door and waiting for him to call me in. After a few seconds I knocked again and pushed the door open. The room was illuminated by the ceiling light, and Charles was face down on the bed, still fully clothed.

'I've brought some tea,' I said. He turned completely round in the bed, ending face down again.

'Charles? Are you all right?'

'Hazel,' he said, turning on to his back and lashing out wildly with his arms. 'Don't go.'

I placed the tea tray on a desk by the window and sat on the edge of the bed. There was a smell of sickness. His eyes were closed. His face was burning.

'I'm going to get you undressed,' I told him. He muttered something about the freezing cold, but he did not know what was happening.

I managed to undress him and made him as comfortable as possible. Then I rang the surgery. I sat by the bed until the doctor arrived. Charles was delirious, calling out for Hazel and his mother, complaining about the weather, sweating freely, and shaking with cold.

The doctor said Charles's fever would continue for some hours, that he would be weak for a few days. He gave me a prescription and left the house, slamming the front door behind him.

Tor awoke and started to cry. I went to his cot and he crouched away from me in the far corner. 'I want Charles,' he said.

'Charles is not very well at the moment,' I said. 'Shall I get you a drink? Or something to eat?'

'I want Charles,' he said. 'And Hazel.'

He started to cry, and struggled when I tried to lift him from the cot. Christine began whimpering from the other side of the room. I took Tor out of the room, closing the door quietly behind us, hoping that Christine would sleep.

'No,' he was yelling, hitting out at my hand and face with his little fists. 'I want Charles and Hazel.' I tried to turn the fight into a joke, pretending to duck his punches, and at the same time talking quickly about how exciting it was to get up in the middle of the night and drink red juice in the kitchen. He gradually quietened down as he realised there was no danger, and the situation might be to his advantage.

'Strong juice,' he said. 'Warm. With sugar in.'

I followed the instructions, pouring it into one of the plastic cups I had seen used earlier. He pointed out that I had used Christine's cup, and that was the best way to spread germs. I transferred it to the other cup, which was identical to the first. I tried to put him at ease by acting the part of a funny man, but he was not to be drawn in that way. He observed me in silence, his face small and white, his eyes betraying nothing of his thoughts.

When I suggested that he should go back to bed, he agreed, but explained that his nappy was wet and I would have to change it. He showed me where the clean nappies were kept, and by trial and error I eventually managed it to his satisfaction. He went quietly to bed, allowing me to tuck the blankets around him; and when I looked into the room ten minutes later he was fast asleep.

Charles was still burning, but he had stopped tossing about and seemed as though he might sleep through the night. I washed and went to bed myself, wondering what the morning would bring.

The next three days were an initiation into fatherhood, or motherhood, or both. Charles tried to get out of bed the first morning and collapsed on the floor. His pyjamas and sheets were wet with perspiration, and I had to change everything before I could start on the children. Their clothes were wet too, my first attempt at putting a nappy on had not been too successful. By the time I had dressed them both, a job that took more than an hour that first morning, I had a pile of wet sheets and pyjamas to fill the washing machine.

Breakfast was chaos. The children had to have their own dishes which were submerged beneath a sink full of dirty pots. There was only a handful of cornflakes left in the box, and I had to fill them up on bread and jam and red juice. Christine dropped everything on the floor, all the time gazing at me with wide eyes, as if unable to believe I had happened to them.

There was no time to think. I was a slave to the day, which roared at me from a thousand different directions. Get the medicine for Charles's illness, but first dress the children, find their outdoor clothes, make a shopping list for cornflakes and food for the rest of the day, master the washing machine, find the soap powder, keep the children happy, give Charles something to eat, drink, read, go to the lavatory, change the nappies again, and again. By the time the children were back in bed in the evening the house was wrecked. I tidied away the toys, swept the kitchen floor, hung out the washing in the dark and refilled the washing machine, took a milky drink up to Charles, who was fast asleep. Then I sat at the kitchen table and fell asleep myself.

I woke with a stiff neck at 1.30 in the morning, dragged myself up to bed, and was awoken by Tor at 2.30 for the red juice treatment. Then we slept until 6am, when it started all over again.

On the day of the funeral Charles and I went together, leaving the children in the care of a neighbour. Charles was still weak from his illness, and I had forfeited so much sleep that I found it difficult to concentrate on the service. There was a dim beauty about it, and an overwhelming sense of accomplishment in the slow descent of the coffin. Like a reluctant soldier, I could have wished that it was not so, but there was a sense of destiny in my participation. Afterwards we exchanged greetings with Hazel's family, with old friends. But there was not much to say. Hazel had gone. We had seen her off.

Charles went back to bed after the service, and I coped with the children for the rest of the day. In the evening I sat with Charles and he asked about the future.

'You wouldn't think of staying on?' he said.

'For a few more days. Until you're fit.'

'No. I mean for the foreseeable future.'

I shook my head.

'It would solve a lot of problems,' he said. 'Tor and Christine are very close. They would both suffer if we split them up. And we could share the load if there were two of us.'

'It wouldn't work, Charles.'

'Do you still intend to take Tor away?'

'That's why I'm here,' I told him. 'I can see it will have to be done gradually. I don't want to cause any more trauma. I can only play it by ear.'

'What's the plan then?' he said.

There wasn't one. 'I don't know. I'll stay for a few more days, and then try to find a flat close by. I want to introduce the idea to Tor gradually. Eventually we'll go back to Norway, or find somewhere in England.'

He shook his head. 'OK. But you don't have to rush anything. You can stay here as long as you like.'

I never seriously looked for another flat. The following week Charles went back to his job with the Council, while I stayed at home with the children. There was plenty to do. The idea of moving out of the house gradually faded away, and I found myself adapting to the role of mother and housewife. Once I tackled Tor about coming to Norway with me, and he seemed to think about it for a long time. Then he said, 'With Christine? And Charles?'

'No,' I said. 'We could visit them sometimes. And sometimes they could visit us. But we wouldn't live in the same house.'

He didn't like the idea.

'We could live in a house by the sea,' I told him. 'And in the winter there would be lots of snow.'

'No,' he said. 'I want to live with Christine. And Charles.'

In the mornings I prepared breakfast while Charles dressed the children. Then he went off to work. I washed the dishes, cleaned the house. Together with the children I did the shopping. After lunch we played games. I read them stories. Then we made dinner together, in time for Charles coming home from work.

Charles and I took it in turns to wash the dinner pots and put the children to bed. And in the evening we played chess or watched the television. Occasionally one or other of us would go to the cinema, and once we hired a babysitter and went to the theatre together. A year went by like that. I enjoyed being with the children during the day, and I appreciated Charles's company in the evening. He enjoyed his job with the Council, and was happy to relax with me when he came home. During the summer we took the kids to the seaside or into the country during the weekends.

Life was uncomplicated, and yet not without meaning. I had had enough of misery, of living close to madness. Charles and I had our fights occasionally, but we always managed to sort them out. I was constantly impressed by how easy he was to live with. He never sat down if there was something to do. And if everything seemed to be getting on top of me he would make a cup of tea, or take over my jobs for a time.

I didn't make his life so easy. I have always been moody, and too easily slip into depression. Sometimes when he returned from work I had barely started on the dinner, and he would roll his sleeves up and start washing carrots or boiling the rice. Other times the kids would be too much during the day, and I would nag about how easy it was for him, while here I was slaving away at the stove, or the washing, talking in babytalk from morning till night.

But he was strong. He managed it all. He would smooth away my depression, undermine my bad moods, and generally make life possible. He was a good man.

4

I destroyed the letter, but I can recall the wording verbatim. It was left on the desk in his bedroom.

Dear Trond,

It would have been painful for both of us to talk about the contents of this letter, and it would have solved no problems. The outcome would have been the same.

Quite simply, I have formed a relationship with someone else, a woman (you don't know her) who needs me, and who I could not consider giving up for anything.

We are going away together (by the time you read this we shall have gone), and I am leaving you with both of the children. Tor and Christine. I hope and pray that you will care for them both.

Best wishes,
Charles

It was written on blue paper in Charles's large handwriting. On the envelope it said: To Trond. And he had propped it up against a stapler on his desk. His cupboard was empty. The drawers of the desk had been cleared. A picture had gone from the wall. The bed had been made.

I walked from the room as though it was possible to leave it behind. To close the door on his bedroom and seal inside the letter and the knowledge of the letter, the act and its implications.

But my will collapsed as I descended the stairs. My legs started to give, and I had to sit on the bottom step. I remember thinking that I wasn't breathing, and was having to take in great gulps of air. I thought, without any hint of panic, that I was dying. The physical processes of my body were no longer being driven.

'What are you doing?' Tor asked, sitting next to me on the step, resting his head on my leg.

'Sitting down,' part of me answered, the other part thinking that perhaps it was a joke, and that even if it wasn't a joke, Charles would regret leaving us and come back again. Yes, tonight; tonight or tomorrow he would come back. Christine was his daughter. We were a family. He couldn't leave us. He couldn't disappear.

'On the stairs?' said Tor.

'Yes. With you.'

'Christine's in the fridge.' He pulled me by the hand and took me into the kitchen. Christine was sitting in front of the open door of the fridge, drinking yoghurt from a carton. The remains of last night's meal were littered on the floor around her.

None of us have seen or heard from Charles since.

Our house by the sea in Oslo is a large, old, wooden building. During the summer we spent a lot of time on the beach, fishing, playing with buckets and spades. Now it is winter and the children are in bed. Today we walked on the frozen surface of the fjord and I can see its silvery sheen from my window as I write the concluding words of this defence.

I do not dwell. I have found an equilibrium in my soul. The two children with whom I live cannot help but remind me of the two adults with whom I lived in England, but they are faded memories, dead memories. At night they come to me in dreams, strangely intermingled with each other. Hazel turns and in a moment of metamorphosis she is Charles. He speaks to me from the other end of a long room, receding as I try to reach him, slowly becoming my faithless wife of long ago.

They are not bad dreams. They do not enlighten me, but they have nothing of the quality of nightmare. The night is beyond me. What happens in the region of sleep is of another world.

But the days are mine. They belong to me and the children. Tor speaks fluent Norwegian now, and Christine has learnt to run and laugh at the same time. I was beginning to think the period of exile was over.

I would dispute that the human remains found under the floorboards of the house in England are those of Charles. But if there is forensic evidence suggesting that the body parts did once belong to him, then it must also be possible to prove that his death took place after we left the country. I must say, without, I hope, appearing macabre, that the missing head is intriguing. Do the British police think that I kept it as a trophy?

I understand that the terms of the extradition treaty between the two countries state that I will have to face the British legal authorities by next year at the latest. But I throw myself upon the mercy of the Norwegian government by means of this full and frank statement of the facts.

Cath Staincliffe

DEATH IN THE AIR

She is dead. I don't need to feel her pulse to work that out. The way she is lying says it all: head against the hearth, legs askew, slack jaw. No trace of movement. An hour previously we'd been talking on the phone. Now this.

I want to run but my knees have gone soft. I gulp air, steady my breathing, try to calm my rising panic: skittering inside like a living thing. I kneel to take her pulse, just in case. She hasn't got one anymore. Her wrist is lukewarm.

It's not your fault, I tell myself.

Oh, no? She was my client.

Only just.

Oh, stop dithering and ring the police.

I do. Then take stock of the situation. She is dressed casually, jog pants and top, parka, trainers. Ready to leave the house. Younger than I'd expected. Glossy black hair, creamy complexion. Eyes closed. Wonder what colour they are? I'm glad she isn't looking at me. No make-up. A faint blue tinge edging her lips. The strong scent of sandalwood, a peppery smell I'd never liked much. Not on her though, must be potpourri. She smells of Lux soap and urine.

On the mantelpiece her purse and keys. I sort through the purse. Organ-donor card, her sister's name and phone number to notify in case of accident. I copy it down. Manchester Leisure Pass with her photo on. She had brown eyes.

The room is neat and tidy. Blue and cream. Ikea by the look of it. No signs of a scuffle. Nothing of interest in the small kitchen. The bedroom is a tip, complete contrast. Clothes strewn on every surface: towels, carrier bags, magazines. The sweet smell of baby powder. Next to the bed a carrycot-cum-crib. Beside it a bag with nappy changing stuff. Giddy again, I steady myself against the bed. The stripey duvet cover ripples then stops.

You don't have to look.

But then I'll never know.

Let the police do it.

I'll always wonder...

I crouch down by the carrycot and peer in. My vision blurs and I shake my head to clear it. A small head, white crocheted hat. Still as stone. I concentrate hard to make my hand move closer to the baby. My stomach tightens, blood beats fast. I stroke a cheek with my finger. The infant stirs, sighs, settles. I breathe again.

Loud banging on the door. My heart hammers, skin prickles with adrenalin. The police are here.

While some of them set about their work I'm in the kitchen being interviewed by the sergeant. I tell him everything I know. It doesn't amount to much.

Julie Willshaw rang me at eight o'clock that evening. We'd never met. She'd got my name from Yellow Pages: 'Sal Kilkenny Investigations, Complete Confidentiality, Free Advice, Female Investigators Available.' There aren't actually any male detectives, it's a one-woman show but I don't advertise the fact.

Julie was panicky and a little incoherent. She said she was being watched by a man, he drove a red car, a Fiesta. She first noticed him at the beginning of the week, he'd been there every evening. She'd no idea what he wanted. She was frightened. Would I find out what was going on? Could I come and see her? She gave me the address. I told her I'd be happy to take the case but I'd prefer her to come to me. It wasn't my policy to go visiting unknown clients, certainly not on dark winter nights. She was reluctant. I persuaded her to call a taxi. She rang off. She never said anything about the baby.

I waited. She didn't show. I began to worry. I heard the fear rising in her voice. Had he been outside as we talked? It got the better of me. I asked my house-mate Ray to stay in and listen for the kids, promised to be back soon. Thursdays was his regular night out.

I doused my old mini-van with WD40 and chugged across the south side of town to Chorlton. On the way I rehearsed the speech I'd make when I found out she'd simply changed her mind. I parked outside the house, no sign of any red Fiesta.

I found the front door slightly ajar, the flat unlocked and my most recent client dead.

It is nearly ten thirty by the time the sergeant has done with me. Now I start feeling guilty about Ray; his Thursday nights are sacrosanct. I drive home quickly. It's a sharp, clear night: frost glinting on the pavements, brick walls washed tangerine by the street lamps; a bloated moon, its face heavy with sorrow, silvers the rooftops.

As I pull into the drive Ray sweeps out muttering something about last orders. I've no chance to explain. What the hell does he think I've been doing? A jaunt up to the peaks? An impulsive trip to the flicks? I do some muttering of my own.

I peek into the kids' room. Maddie lays spread-eagled on top of the covers, completely relaxed. Tom, in his cot, sleeps with his bum in the air. The image of Julie Willshaw's baby returns. All alone. Suddenly I am shaking, I'm so cold. Tears sting my eyes. Delayed shock. It's my first dead body. One is more than enough. I've been investigating for eighteen months. I started off on the Enterprise Allowance Scheme. The training didn't run to situations like this.

Sometime in the depths of a fretful night I know I can't let it rest there. Julie wanted me to find out who was watching her. She died before she could tell me more. Who is the man in the red Fiesta? Some psycho staking her out? Or someone with a score to settle? Was it luck that she landed against the hearth? Had he come with a knife or a gun and not needed it? Or was it simply an accident? Almost ready to leave, had she stumbled and fallen? Did she fall or was she pushed? The thoughts spin through my mind, over and over like balls in a Tombola, clattering through my dreams. It's a relief to be woken at six o'clock by Maddie claiming to be starving hungry as anything.

With the kids deposited at play group and nursery I set to work. I ring the number from the organ-donor card: Julie's sister, Elaine Hattersley. I explain directly who I am and why I want to talk to her. The honest approach works.

Elaine could be the spitting image of her sister except for the fact that she is ten years older, ten years tireder and full of grief. She has a swollen nose and puffy eyes from too much crying. She is chain smoking as we talk. Her two toddlers are watching telly, one of them comes over and lays his head on her lap, comforting her for a moment before wandering back to his spot on the carpet. In the corner sits the carrycot. The baby is fine. Elaine will take him if they'll let her.

'She loved that kid,' her mouth quivers.

I nod. Listen as she talks about the baby. Wait for a pause to start my questions.

'Julie told me she was being watched, someone in a red car was parked outside her place.'

'Yeah,' Elaine sighs, stubs out her cigarette, 'she told me but... don't get me wrong but she were very nervy, always strung out, even as a kid. And after she had Sam she got depressed. You know how it is, no sleep, she were on her own with him, yer mind starts playing tricks on you. The doctor put her on tablets...'

'You thought she was imagining it?'

'I don't know. Not now. I said to her, who'd want to watch you? Maybe it was the other flats upstairs, or the neighbours he was watching.' She shakes her head. 'I keep thinking I should've listened.'

She fumbles for a fresh cigarette, clicks her lighter, eyes screwed up against the smoke. The first smell of burning tobacco curls my way.

'The police aren't sure whether anyone was there or not,' she says, 'they reckon she could have fallen, tripped over.'

Could her medication have made her unsteady?

'They said until they have the results... and even then...' Her eyes glitter with tears, she takes a deep drag on the cigarette.

'Was Julie involved with anybody?'

'Not recently,' she exhales.

'Who was the baby's father?'

'Bloke called Peter Dalton,' another drag, 'he was no good for her. Married, always promising to leave his wife.'

'He wasn't still seeing her?'

'No. Packed it in last summer. Good riddance to bad rubbish. Mind you, I'd have been the last to know if he was. She knew what I thought.'

'Does he drive a red car?'

She shrugs, blows her nose.

'Where does he live?'

'Dunno, Stockport way I think. But he works at that big computer place near the Apollo, you know where I mean?'

Leaving Elaine's I make my way back to Julie's flat. No sign of police activity. The terrace house is divided into three. No one answers the top bell but I strike lucky with the middle one. I explain who I am to Ranjana Mehta. She is happy to talk to me. She has already been interviewed by the police. She makes tea for us and we sit at the round table in the bay window. The room is chilly. I can smell the apples in the fruit bowl. I clutch the mug tight, warming my hands. I tell her about Julie's phone call. Did Ranjana see the man in the red car?

'Yes, I did. I hadn't thought anything of it until Julie told me about it and then I realised the car had been there a lot, in the evenings. I'd seen the bloke get out and go up to the corner shop one time. It never occurred to me he might be watching

the house, or Julie or whatever. You see these people sitting in
cars and you never think what are they up to. Well, I never do,'
she pulls a face, screws her nose up.

'When did Julie talk to you about it?'

'Yesterday. I was on my way to college. She was in quite a
state. Said he'd been watching her, she was really scared.'

'The man you saw, what did he look like?'

'The police asked me, I can't remember much. Short, bit on
the fat side, blond hair,' she nods reassuring herself that she has
it right, 'he wore a leather jacket, a smart one.'

'Was he here at all last night?'

'I don't know. I didn't get back till eleven.'

'Was he there when Julie asked you about him?'

'No. I never saw him in the daytime.'

'Just evenings?'

'Yes.'

'Since when?'

'Julie thought it started at the weekend. I'm pretty sure he
was there every night this week, anyway.'

'Did there seem to be particular times?'

'I'm sorry, I didn't pay that much attention.'

'Had Julie any regular visitors?'

'Just her boyfriend. You'd think he'd have done something,
ask this bloke what he was up to...' She takes a drink.

'Her boyfriend?'

'Peter, he was here on Wednesday night.'

'I heard they'd split up.'

Ranjana shrugs. 'Could have fooled me.'

'Have you any idea why Julie was being watched. Had there
ever been any trouble?'

'No, nothing. I did wonder if it might be the DSS, when she
told me about it, or the Child Support Agency. Snoopers, you
know. They could cut her benefit if they thought Peter was
supporting her or make him pay maintenance for the baby.'

'Was he supporting her?'

'I don't know. We weren't that close. Anyway now she's... well it's not likely to be the DSS is it?' She drains her cup.

I agree. Some of them are pretty nasty but there are limits.

'The police said it may just have been an accident. No connection to the bloke in the red car.' There's a note of strained hope in her voice. I don't blame her. Who wants to believe that another woman has been slain under the same roof. 'What do you think?' she asks me.

'I don't know.'

But I'm sure the two things are connected. I'm not one for astonishing coincidences. I just don't know how they are connected. Not yet.

Tom is eating his lunch. He brought home a picture of an umbrella from playgroup. I pin it on the board. While he is busy with his marmite sandwich I ring the firm where Peter Dalton, Julie's boyfriend, works. Luckily I get a dozy receptionist who informs me Mr Dalton has gone home. I tell her I am an old friend visiting from New Zealand, in town for the day. The old number I had for Peter isn't working, can I check it with her. I reel off a number and she checks her files. No, this is the new one. I write it down. He's still in Stockport, I ask, and she reels off the address too. Saving me the bother of getting it from the phone book. Presumably she hasn't heard that his mistress has been found dead.

Tom and I are sticking pasta shapes to paper. I am thinking about Julie. What will they tell the baby when he's bigger? Will they let Elaine keep him? Do relatives have any priority in adopting these days? I tell Tom to finish off. We have to go get Maddie from nursery school. Ray will be back from college about four thirty. And I can get back to work.

Peter Dalton's house boasts a double garage and a monkey puzzle tree. Both a little grand for the Edwardian semi on the Stockport border. The man himself answers the door. Tall, thin, balding. Bags under his eyes, droopy eyes like a spaniel, bloodshot eyes. Peter Dalton has been crying.

'Yes?' He sounds exhausted.

'I've come about Julie.'

Guilt and embarrassment chase each other across his face.

'Is there somewhere we can talk?'

'Who are you?' He frowns. 'I've already spoken to the police.'

And they haven't arrested him.

'Sal Kilkenny, I'm a private detective. Julie rang me yesterday, she wanted my help. Before I could...'

'You'd better come in,' he says hurriedly. He waves me through into a small study. Points me to an office chair.

'I don't know anything,' he folds himself into an armchair. 'I saw her on Wednesday.'

'Did she tell you she thought someone was watching her?'

'Yes. I'm afraid I didn't pay it much attention. If I'd just...' He looks away, his Adam's apple bobs up and down. 'She had a vivid imagination. Things had got on top of her since Sam...' He covers his mouth with his hand. 'The car was there, she wasn't making that up but I couldn't see why she thought it had anything to do with her. I thought she was getting upset over nothing.'

'The police haven't said yet whether they suspect foul play?'

'No. That makes it worse. Not knowing. If it was... oh, God. You know what I said? "Go back to the doctor, ask him for something stronger to calm you down."' He makes a bitter noise in his throat.

'Does your wife know?'

'That she's dead?' His voice threatens to break. 'No. The police saw me at work first thing this morning. I told Alison that it was all over last summer. She'd no idea... God knows how I'm going to...'

I hear the front door opening.

He sits bolt upright, panic rounding his eyes. 'That'll be her now. Please don't say anything.'

Does he think she won't notice the way he looks?

'Peter? Peter?'

The door opens and Alison Dalton comes in. Medium height, long chestnut brown hair in a loose perm, careful make-up, sunbed tan, smart russet suit.

'There you are... what are you... oh...' She stops short on seeing me.

I get to my feet. I don't know how Peter is going to pass me off. We don't get that far. As soon as Alison enters the room I know exactly what she's done.

'Peter?' She sees the state of him. 'What on earth's the matter?' Perhaps she thinks I'm from the police. She looks at me perplexed, a tiny frown furrows between her eyebrows, confusion clouds her eyes. 'What's happened?' She's very convincing.

'I'm a private detective, Mrs Dalton. I've come about Julie Willshaw. I'm going to ring the police now. You need to talk to them.'

Her face remains composed, only her mouth works silently twisting and quivering beyond her control. 'I haven't the faintest idea what you mean. What is going on?'

'What on earth?' Peter Dalton glances from his wife to me and back again.

'Julie Willshaw, Mrs Dalton.'

'Alison?' Barely a whisper from Peter.

There is a pause. She swallows, presses her lips together, her nostrils widen. She gives a small laugh. 'It was an accident. A silly accident, that's all.'

'Alison,' he repeats and horror sluices across his face like spilt milk. 'No,' his protest is deep, strangled.

'Exactly what did you expect?' She rounds on him, spits the words out, hard and caustic. 'You thought you could get away with it again. I'm not stupid, Peter, not like you. You were so obvious; all the overtime, just like before. Very imaginative. I knew. After everything we'd agreed, after all that you went sneaking back, sniffing round...' She chokes on her rage.

172

She steps back, stretches out an arm, jabbing a finger at him.
'I got someone to watch the flat.'

Someone in a red Fiesta.

'He saw you on Wednesday. He told me about the baby.'
There are flecks of spit at the corners of her mouth. 'We agreed
it was over. You promised. We agreed. You never wanted children,' she roars. 'Nothing to come between us.' Were you there
for the birth? Did you choose its name? You bastard,' she
screeches, 'you pathetic bastard.' Now she breaks down, her
mouth stretches with grief, tears splash down her face.

He looks blank, empty. Nobody moves. Then she begins to
speak again, hurried, pleading.

'I only meant to warn her off, tell her you'd never leave me.
She panicked. She tried to leave. She wasn't listening. I had to
make her see sense. She wouldn't listen. She was shouting. I
pushed her, that's all. I just wanted her to be quiet and listen to
me. It wasn't my fault. She should have listened,' she protests,
sounding injured.

She crosses and kneels at his side, grips the arm of the chair
and offers her face up to him. 'One little mistake,' her voice is
small and wheedling, 'it needn't make a difference. We've still
got each other, Peter my love. That's all we need. That's all we
ever needed.'

'Oh, Alison,' his face is a mixture of pity and revulsion. He
starts crying too. Great ugly sobs into his pale, spindly hands.

I ring the police.

They'd have cottoned on pretty quickly, of course. Once the
private investigator that Alison had hired got to hear about Julie
Willshaw's death he would report his assignment.
Confidentiality only stretches so far. I save them a little time,
that's all.

I knew Alison Dalton killed Julie as soon as I met her. She
carried the evidence with her. Proof that she was in the flat that
night. When Alison came into the room something else came
too. The overpowering smell of rich, sandalwood perfume.

Murder Squad

COLLAGE

Although the books we write are very different, we've identified three elements in common: 1 – The Setting. 2 – The Crime. 3 – The Aftermath.

1. The Setting
'Setting' may be used to describe location, character, or the emotional place the characters occupy. But effects in fiction are complex and interconnected – each draws on and contributes to all the others. Physical location is crucial: it determines the mood and atmosphere of the drama.

Hunched figures were spread across the uneven slopes of the waste heap... They wore ancient anoraks or duffel coats, bending double as they shifted through the rubbish that other people had no use for. Most of them wore hoods, one or two had donned balaclavas. They were not mercly, Harry realised, seeking protection against the February wind, but also aiming to avoid recognition if a social security snooper came to check on those claiming benefits from the state. Through the high wire fence, Harry watched the totters at work. He might have been observing a scene from the Third World on television. But this was his home town. This was Liverpool.

(All the Lonely People, Piatkus, 1991)

Not, perhaps, the most comfortable portrayal of Liverpool, but Martin Edwards has produced a true portrait of the deprivation experienced by one section of urban society. Truth is something the author strives for with a fervour akin to obsession. Consider this example from John Baker. Geordie's close (gross?) attention to detail reflects the writer's sometimes unsavoury interest in telling it how it is.

When she came in Geordie thought Marnie was the ugliest woman he'd ever seen in his life. Claude had a beaut of his own, but if anything Marnie's honker was even more obscene. Claude's had a whole network of external veins feeding it, which drew your attention. Marnie didn't have that, what she had was exactly the opposite. Her nose had been starved of blood for a long time, and as a result it was withering away. It was a much darker hue than the rest of her features, being composed almost entirely of blackheads. 'Nearest you could get to a description of it,' Geordie told Janet later, 'was, well it was like something a wasp would make. But not a regular wasp's nest. If you could imagine a wasp that'd always been a failure, a kind of black-sheep wasp. You know what I mean? From a broken home, and a mixed marriage, and it left home too early, before its parents had time to teach it things. Like it would build something like Marnie's nose and try to live in it.

(*King of the Streets*, Victor Gollancz, 1998)

Domestic settings may be used to lighten an otherwise dark novel. Here Ann Cleeves uses the messy reality of everyday life to provide light relief.

Emma saw her pregnancy as an act of rudeness. How inappropriate, how impolite to be blossoming at this time of grief! Brian had invited Mark to stay with them for a few days after the death of his wife and whenever she saw him she felt herself blushing. But then Mark had always possessed the knack of making her feel awkward.

Emma had come to motherhood relatively late and took to it with a passion and energy which surprised her colleagues. They'd expected her back in harness straight after maternity leave. Not for the money. Husband Brian more than provided. But because they couldn't imagine the Human Resources Department without her.

She didn't return to work. She had two boys in quick succession and now she was pregnant again. *Hoping* for a girl, of course, she confided to her new mumsy friends, but happy to take what came. Then Sheena had died sooner than they had expected and the pregnancy seemed some dreadful social gaff.

They left straight after the funeral. It had been Brian's idea to buy the Coastguard Station on the Headland and knock it through into one big house. She hadn't been keen. Even then she'd been dreaming of babies and thought a modern house on a quiet estate would be nice. Somewhere with other middle class mothers to invite in to coffee during the day, pavements for trikes and dolls' prams. Of course the house was wonderful now but the place still made her feel uneasy. There was a high white-washed wall but she worried that the children would fall. Some nights she would wake up sweating to a picture of one of them limp and lifeless at the foot of the cliff.

The car jolted across the level crossing and she saw with relief that they were nearly home.

… At the house she struggled out of the car with difficulty. She loved being pregnant but would be glad when it was all over. She was standing on the doorstep, rummaging in her bag for her keys, when her waters broke.

'Oh God!' Brian said with a trace of disgust when she explained what had happened. Both thought with relief that at least it hadn't happened when she was getting out of the car. Think of the leather upholstery.

(*The Baby Snatcher*, Macmillan, 1997)

From the cliffs of Northumberland to the towering mills of Cath Staincliffe's Manchester: a man-made landscape, shattered by human destructiveness.

There's no point in driving into town on a Saturday. Parking's difficult to find and outrageously expensive into the bargain. I got the bus into Piccadilly Gardens. It was a few minutes walk down Market Street to the Corn Exchange.

Traffic was snarling up around the terminus and there seemed to be a lot of police vans around. As I reached the top of Market Street I ran into a crowd of people. I thought there'd been an accident or maybe a robbery. The police helicopter flew overhead very low down. I turned to ask the man next to me if he knew what was going on.

Before he could answer, there was a great bang. Then nothing. A gust of air. I felt a surge in my stomach. A blast of wind and dust, strong enough to affect my balance. A cloud of smoke plumed into the sky. I thought I could hear screaming, lots of screaming. It was a chorus of alarms, shrilling and screeching.

They'd bombed the Arndale Centre.

(Dead Wrong, Headline, 1997)

We all love a loveable rogue, especially when he brings a touch of humour to a grim situation.

He'd parked in Hope Street, round the corner from the Liverpool Institute of Performing Arts – what everyone called the Fame School. Uphill all the way. Even with a following wind from the Mersey, he'd broken out into a sweat within minutes and he felt his wheeze coming on. At the corner of Mount Street, one of the regular prozzies had turned out early, hoping to catch a bit of white collar custom on their way home from the office.

'Got the time, lad?' she asked.

'I might have the time, but I wouldn't bet on having the energy, girl,' Lobo said, trying to control the harshness of his breathing.

'I'll give you chance to catch your breath,' she said, following him a few steps from the corner. 'No extra charge.'

Lobo shook his head and hurried on. They embarrassed him, the street girls, even though this one had a nice pair of legs and he would've liked to try her out, if he'd had the nerve. But he was frightened of diseases, a weakness Lee-Anne played on every opportunity she could, quoting facts and figures from her magazines, telling him about the threat of AIDS and syphilis; bloody bitch even took him to see *The Madness of King George*, and for weeks she kidded him on old George'd gone off his head 'cos of some venereal disease or other. Oh, she knew his weak spots, Lee-Anne did.

(Margaret Murphy, *Past Reason*, Macmillan, 1998)

2. The Crime

The crime can be planned and the plans may work, or they may be undermined. Conversely, there may be no plan at all, or only a vague intimation of one thing that leads to another. Sometimes the crime is almost accidental, the confluence of circumstance and character. Here the girls are out on the town.

So we're waiting bleedin' ages for a bus. I'm the only one with any fags left and they're all tapping off me and I'm dying for a drink but we haven't even got enough for a can of Coke. The bus says West Didsbury. Kelly says it's okay, next to Didsbury and she's sure there's loads of students there. I think maybe it'll change. Next half-hour. All come right. One or two hits and we'll be sorted. Money in us pockets, grinning wide, ready to roll. Into town for a long cold drink and a Big Mac and on to some serious shopping. Made up.

We get off the bus and we're going down this side street,

quiet. Lots of trees again. Massive they are, dead old. Hiding the houses. Make the sun look softer. How come there's no trees like that round our way? Just weedy little ones that the kids bend over, snap off?

No one about. I don't know where the fuck we are any more. It's that hot. This is no fun. This is not my idea of easy money. I just want to go home and get a bleedin' drink.

I tell Becca, 'Let's go home. This is stupid.'

He comes out of one of the driveways. Smallish guy, black hair, white T-shirt, black jeans, crap trainers.

'Scuse me.' Becca makes it sound like a threat.

'Yes, how can I help you girls?' Perky like. Not posh. Ferrety face. Gold cross in one ear. Gay? Catholic? Both?

'Empty your pockets.' Becca says. He shakes his head grinning.

'Aw, come on now...'

'Just do it, fuckin' do it.' Becca is totally still.

Do it, I'm thinking, do what she says, please.

He lifts his hands up like it's a Western and he's surrendering. He has spatula fingers, flat and wide at the end. They look babyish on him. 'I've no more money than you, ya know.' Becca doesn't even enter the argument. She pulls a blade from her pocket, flicks it open and slices it across his throat. That quick. Smooth as silk.

His hands flutter and a crease of red splits across his neck. He's still smiling and he looks at me. Straight at me. Soft, puzzled. Like Mam did when the baby died.

(Cath Staincliffe, *The City Life Book of Manchester Short Stories*, City Life and Penguin, 1999)

Tense and point-of-view can also be employed to narrate the scene of a crime. Chaz Brenchley uses second-person narration to bring us up close, almost inside the head of a criminal who sees the world in isolation.

Inside your bag, something shifts with a cold sound as you turn into the road beside the river. You smile, and heft the bag in your hand, feeling the weight of it.

There are benches along the quayside; and he's waiting at one of them, as he promised. He sits hunched and alone, staring out over the water, almost in the shadow of the bridge.

He glances up as you get closer. He's a younger man, probably in his early twenties. His hair hangs limply to his shoulders, and his cheeks look half-molten in the alien light. Acne, perhaps – the vicious kind that comes with adolescence and stays till middle-age.

'Hullo,' he says dully, knowing you, his voice flat and bitter, a salt plain with no water. 'Thanks for coming.'

You nod and drop the bag beside the bench. It settles heavily, and you smile again, thinking of hooks, and of rope. Chain would perhaps have been better; but there was none in the garage, and you were in a hurry. Next time, perhaps – though next time, of course, it will be different.

You sit down beside the boy, murmuring something about the river, and the night. He only grunts in reply, but that's all right. This is a game you've played many times, and you know the rules. There's more than one way to open a conversation, and one of the best is to say nothing.

Waiting, you watch the boy as he lights a cigarette with shaking hands. He's thin, harsh-edged against the city's glow, coarse-featured and afraid. You look at his wrists, slender like a woman's; at his bony shoulders; at his neck, jutting out of an upturned collar. You count imaginary vertebrae between your fingers, like a rosary.

It would be so simple, so laughably simple. You could reach out, grip him so, twist thus – and it would be done. You could do it for him, as you did it for… as you did it, once before.

But let him talk, there's no hurry. And there's no need to be so quick yourself. You've learned that. All roads lead to Rome; so what does it matter, if some of them are slower and less easy? It means nothing in the end. How could it?

So you sit back, ready to listen; but your mind is playing already with rope, and with hooks; and your eyes are straying to the iron girders of the bridge above...

(*The Samaritan*, Hodder & Stoughton, 1988)

Stuart Pawson provides more than an example of the kind of humour that is often associated with the genre. The word 'Burlesque' comes to mind.

Sex in unusual places has its own eroticism, but it does sometimes fall down on practicality. Vicky was lying entirely within the borders of the rug, with its woven pattern of scarab beetles, but Lee's feet projected beyond it, on to the parquet floor, which the ladies of the congregation polished, with assiduity and Johnson's Wax, every Tuesday morning.

He was wearing Reebok basketball boots, famed for their grip on slippery surfaces. Every thrust of his loins pushed Vicky and the rug across the floor, and every three or four thrusts his toes stuttered forwards to bring him back into the optimum position. Slowly they progressed across the vestry, like some gothic, ratchet-propelled beast.

It was unsatisfactory for Vicky, too. She flailed her arms around, trying to find a fixture to cling to. There was nothing at all within the arc of her right arm, but the left was underneath the big wooden desk.

She groped about in vain for several seconds, then she thought her fingertips brushed something. The next thrust confirmed her thoughts and the one after that brought it within her grasp.

Vicky grabbed hold and braced herself, but it wasn't the solid anchorage she was hoping for. It was soft and yielding, as well as wet and sticky.

It was another hand.

Vicky gasped with terror and yanked her own hand back. She

held it above her and blood dripped from it onto her face.

Her scream echoed around the high roof and set the starlings flying from the tower. With a mighty convulsion she threw Lee off and jumped to her feet. The locked door delayed her progress slightly, but within seconds she was running barefoot out into the night, still screaming.

Lee had just reached the good bit. Vicky's first recoil action made him think that for once his timing was perfect. He was on the backstroke, on the verge of the big finale, when she shot out from under him and he impregnated a woven scarab beetle with half a billion of his healthy, if genetically undistinguished, spermatazoa.

Exhausted and frustrated, he collapsed on the rug. He was facing the underside of the desk, but his right arm was obscuring his vision. Beyond it, in the shadows, Lee could make-out what looked like somebody's shoulder, wearing a tweed jacket. His hand was trembling uncontrollably as he drew it back, and he found himself staring into the sightless gaze of the late Reverend Ronald Conway.

(*The Mushroom Man*, Headline, 1995)

The crime is sometimes referred to as an aesthetic experience. The perpetrator, often a murderer, regards himself or herself as an artist.

Did he speak? I've been trying to remember – it all happened so fast, slickly, like a movie – there should have been atmospheric music. I think – I *think* – he smiled, no more, smoothed the white linen, laying one hand palm down on the still-warm sheet. The air pregnant with the smell of recent sex; mouth drying, faintly repugnant. Irrefutable.

No struggle, no panic. Only the push of breath, hands gripping the sheets, twisting them – shock at the unexpectedness of it. But the knife had been well-honed with every ritualized rehearsal of his carefully planned death, and it pierced –

dermis, adipose tissue, striated muscle, pericardium, smooth muscle – effortlessly.

Such a small thing, so lightweight, the blade slim, elegant in its way, marked by a thousand tiny striations, sharpened and resharpened in preparation for its work. Strange how one can develop a regard, almost an affection for one's tools – at least if they give good service.

Like a burst balloon, he seemed to collapse in on himself. A failure of pressure. He was dead in seconds. It was humane, almost painless. The small incision, high in his chest, seeping gouts of bright crimson, summoned an image of the crucified Christ.

(Margaret Murphy, *Caging the Tiger*, Macmillan, 1997)

The opening scene of one of Martin Edwards's novels is bloody. There is a gothic feel here, in the tone and pacing of the language. And the horror and suspense of the scene are in direct counterpoint to the final image.

Shaun could not see the bodies, but he knew where they were buried.

The house had once been a church and these grounds were the old graveyard.

The stone walls of the building were stained with soot and the squat tower was adorned with a burglar alarm. Shaun knew the red light would be winking if the alarm had been set. Approaching the porch, he saw the door was ajar.

The temptation was overwhelming and he was in no mood to resist. He pushed at the brass handle and the door swung open with a disconsolate whine.

As he crossed the threshold, he realised that everything was about to go wrong. The place was cold after the heat outside, but it was more than that. The silence was stifling. No unlocked house in the heart of the city should be so quiet or smell so strangely of decay. His throat had dried.

Facing him was an arched entrance with a pair of flung-back doors. Beyond, the vestibule opened out into a vast hall. He inched forward until he stood underneath the arch, then froze. The largest rug he had ever seen stretched across the hall. Once the rug had been beige, but now it was disfigured by dark spreading marks.

The sight of the bodies hit him like a kick in the face. Not all the dead of St Alwyn's were safely underground. There was a great deal of blood, more than any Shaun had ever seen in a midnight movie. He felt his gorge rise and he tried to force his eyes shut, but they refused to close.

Three people were sprawled across the floor. Two of them reached towards each other, as though in the moment of death they had striven to unite in a final embrace. The third, barely alive, mumbled something Shaun could not quite catch and stretched out an arm, seeming to point at an object a couple of feet away. As Shaun began to retch, he saw that the object was a small and sightless furry animal. A young child's toy teddy bear. (*Eve of Destruction*, Piatkus, 1996)

3. The Aftermath

Every murder has its aftermath: the shock waves that ripple out, the reverberations that transform the lives of those left behind and sound a challenge to those who wish to bring the killer to light. Here Margaret Murphy explores that terrifying freeze-frame moment which signals the transition from one state of affairs to another, the moment when the truth hurtles towards us like a juggernaut.

'Once more, on pain of death, all men depart.'

Liam finished his speech with a flourish.

'Good,' Geri said. 'Now before we move on to poor, love-sick Romeo' – she got the expected groan at this – 'Who can tell me what the last speech was about?'

... A sharp rap at the classroom door announced Mrs Golding. All eyes turned to the plump, grey-haired woman in the doorway. The look on her face was enough: she had come for Dean. He was slouched across his desk, one arm flung out to the side, his head resting on it. When he saw Mrs Golding he sat upright, watching her as if she were a snake about to strike.

'Miss,' he said, watching the deputy head, but talking to Geri. 'He's telling them off.'

'Dean...' Mrs Golding said. She had a sharp, businesslike manner, but she knew when to be gentle.

''Cos they're always at it, fighting and that, bickering back and forth, Miss –' The urgency in his voice turning to desperation.

'Dean –'

'The lads wanna prove they're hard, so they're always looking for a ruck, taking offence – say it's a nice day, they'll ask if you're being funny.'

Geri and Mrs Golding exchanged a dismayed glance.

'And the old one's wanna prove they aren't past it. It's just... mad.'

He carried on with furious concentration, gritting his teeth and hunching his shoulders, talking faster and faster. 'So he's telling them they've had it this time. It's their last chance. Anyone else gets caught at it, they're dead.' He flinched at this word, and went on, as if trying to take it back: 'When I say *dead*, I mean they're in big trouble, 'cos it's not safe to walk the streets, with them sword-fighting and –'

Geri walked over to him and placed one hand on his shoulder. He fell silent and looked at her as if she had done him a mortal injury.

'It's all right, Dean,' she said. 'Mrs Golding will look after you.'

Dean walked to the front of the class, watched in silence by the others. He looked incredibly small and fragile. His breathing rasped in the silence, and he turned back to Geri as if expecting her to rescue him. He shuddered as Mrs Golding touched his arm. She looked over at Geri. Whatever had happened, it was worse, much worse than she had imagined. She understood his reluctance to leave: while he remained in class, while he remained ignorant, he could imagine anything at all – that Ryan was off somewhere enjoying himself, oblivious to the concern he was causing – But going with Mrs Golding would change all that: he would be presented with the unavoidable, irrevocable truth.

'Thank you, Nine S,' Mrs Golding said retreating into brisk formality. 'You can carry on now.'

No, Geri thought. *We can't. We really can't.* She stared at the anxious faces of her form and they stared back. A line kept running through her head, *Oh where is Romeo? – saw you him today?* (*Dying Embers*, Macmillan, 1999)

In many narratives, suspicion, evidence and investigation build up to the chase, the hunt to catch the quarry. Ann Cleeves's middle-aged detective Vera Stanhope is in her element.

There was no movement until dusk and then it was cautious, giving the impression of an animal coming out after dark to drink.

Deliberately, slowly, Vera laced her boots. Outside it was still warm, the air smelling of sweet gorse and crushed bracken. As she walked onto the hill her eyes got used to the grey light, the hazy shapes.

She was loving every minute of it. She thought this must be how Hector and Connie felt when they raided the Lake District Golden Eagles, sneaking up to the site, knowing the warden was dossing nearby in his tent and the police had promised regular patrols. They did it for this buzz.

Christ, she thought. I must be light headed. Thinking I can understand that pair. That's what's exercise does for you. And having nothing to eat all day except a packet of biscuits.

The woman was in the old engine house standing with her back to the gap in the wall. She wore a long skirt over boots. She had loosened a flagstone from the corner of the room and shifted it enough so she could dig out the soil underneath. The grave must have been shallow because already Vera saw a fragment of bone, cream as ivory, waxy in the candlelight. The woman squatted and began to scrabble at the soil with her fingers.

Suddenly behind Vera, so close it was like a scream, there was a cry of exclamation. The woman in the building stood and turned in one movement, giving a throaty growl of astonishment. Then she ran and seemed to disappear.

A second later the scene was hit like a stage by the spot of Ashworth's flashlight.

'Did anyone pass you?'

'No.'

'I think I know where she's heading. Friendly territory.'

As she walked off she could hear him shouting at her not to be so bloody stupid, that this was no time to play cops and robbers. But the words seemed very distant. She turned back once to him.

'Look, I know what I'm doing. This is friendly territory for me too.'

But he was still shouting, his mouth opening and shutting in the torchlight and she didn't know whether or not he'd heard.

(*The Crow Trap*, Macmillan, 1999)

Often the pursuit is successful. This is Detective Inspector Charlie Priest bringing in his man.

When the sobbing subsided I grabbed a handful of Gore-Tex and hoisted him to his feet. 'Walk!' I ordered. He stumbled a few feet and sank to his knees. I yanked him up again and kicked him.'Walk!' I yelled. 'Walk! Walk! Walk!'

We made slow progress. When dawn broke, bright and new,

we were only halfway along Swirral Edge. Kingston fell to the ground and said he could go no further. I grabbed him by the throat and stuffed the end of the CS canister into his left nostril. 'Get this,' I hissed at him. 'You can either walk out of here or you can be carried. But if I have to carry you the first thing I'll do is empty this up your friggin' nose. So get up on your feet and *walk*!'

After that we made better progress. On the bridle path leading into Patterdale a group of hikers approached us. They were all fairly elderly, out to enjoy a day on the fells. As we reached them Kingston turned to one, his shackled wrists held forward in an appeal for help. I grabbed his arm and steered him past them with a communal *Good morning*. They all turned to watch us go by, mumbling their greetings, not believing their eyes. This was the Lake District, after all. When we were past them the first one to recover her senses called 'What's he done?' after us.

'Dropped a crisp packet,' I muttered without looking back.

(Stuart Pawson, *Some by Fire*, Headline, 1999)

Following sudden violent death we find ourselves in no-man's-land: friends, family, lovers negotiating unexpected, unfamiliar territory.

And when she got to the bench and sat down with Celia next to her she knew her life had changed for ever and Gus was dead and with him had gone all the dreams and plans of a lifetime. And in one way her life up to this point had been a complete lie, because nothing that had been dreamed in it would ever now come to fruition. And then in another way, in lots of ways, more than she could think of, her life had not even begun, never begun. Not until now. On this small wooden bench in the police station she was born.

Then Geordie came through the door in his leather jacket with the bullet hole in the back, and he looked confused as well. And shortly after him came Sam, with the man who was a solicitor, and whose name Marie couldn't remember, but thought might be Forester. And Sam came over to the bench and went down on his knees in front of her, and his face was also wet with tears. Sam Turner, the big constant.

Crying like a man.

Marie was a nurse and knew pain and tears. Men didn't know how to cry. When they lost control they felt guilty and the original motivation for the tears got lost. That's why they made a noise about it. And that's why it was such a job to get them to stop.

(John Baker, *Death Minus Zero*, Victor Gollancz, 1996)

While for the characters involved in the bloody act, whether attacking or defending, a whole gamut of reactions follow. Not least fear of the consequences. Here private eye Sal Kilkenny fears the worst.

I'd lost all sense somewhere in the fear and the bleeding, and the only thing that occurred to me was to walk until I found someone.

I set off jogging slowly down the narrow road. It was laid with white gravel, like the stones that Hansel dropped. I wanted to lie down and sleep. I wanted to hide somewhere far away where they'd never find me. Guilt. Fear.

To the rhythm of my steps I chanted a mantra: Don't let him die, please, don't let him die.

He may have been a grade A dickhead but I didn't want to be his murderer.

(Cath Staincliffe, *Go Not Gently*, Headline, 1997)

And as our stories conclude, the police, private investigators, amateurs or reluctant participants are invariably challenged and changed themselves by the journey they make. It is their shoes we have borrowed, their view we have admitted and the account of their travels is as important as any revelation of exactly who did what and why. Martin Edwards's protagonist Harry Devlin has completed the case and now faces the end of an ill-fated affair with a gangster's wife that almost cost him his life.

'It's an obsession with you,' Juliet said. 'The need to discover the truth – whatever the cost. But sometimes the price is too high to be worth paying.'

'Maybe I need counselling,' he said, trying to make a joke of it. 'Ever come across someone who specialises in Compulsive Detection Syndrome?'

If he'd hoped she would laugh, he was disappointed. 'I ought to tell you,' she said. 'Casper's been appointed to the north west task force on elder care.'

Jesus. A fragment of a song swam into his mind. Hope I die before I grow old.

'Well,' she said, 'I'd better be going. Boycott Duff have given me a marketing brief. The senior partner's a bit miffed about the coverage of Spendlove's death.'

'I thought no publicity was bad publicity?'

'They prefer their partners to die of strokes through over-work. It's difficult to put a positive spin on things when your Head of Corporate Recovery is stripped, stabbed and then thrown in the water to drown.'

'Think of it as a challenge.'

'They want to reposition themselves in the legal market-place. They are increasing their commitment to free advice for the underclass. Sharks in Samaritans' clothing is the only slogan I've come up with so far. A tad more work needed yet, I'm afraid. See you around, Harry.'

'Sure,' he said. His stomach was churning. He didn't know whether he would ever see her again. He didn't know whether he wanted to.

(*First Cut Is the Deepest*, Hodder & Stoughton, 1999)

Murder Squad Who's Who

 **John Baker** is the creator of Sam Turner, a gritty private eye based in York, now John's own home after living on the Continent for some time. This series includes *Death Minus Zero, King of the Streets* and *Shooting in the Dark*, and the next is *The Meanest Flood* (Autumn 2002). He has also launched a second series with *The Chinese Girl,* set in Hull and featuring ex-con Stone Lewis. With his interest in ideas, cultural themes and social injustice, John concentrates more on character and content than on plot, but still keeps the pages turning.

 **Chaz Brenchley** is the author of nine thrillers, most recently *Shelter*, and a major fantasy series based on the world of the Crusades, *The Books of Outremer.* A recipient of the British Fantasy Award, he has also published three fantasy books for children and more than 500 short stories. His time as Crime-writer in Residence at the St Peter's Sculpture Project in Sunderland resulted in the collection *Blood Waters.* Recently a writer-in-residence at the University of Northumbria, he lives in Newcastle upon Tyne with two cats and a famous teddy bear.

 **Ann Cleeves** has written two distinct series. In the first an elderly naturalist solves conservation crimes. The second, set in Northumberland, features Detective Inspector Ramsay. Her recent psychological thriller *The Crow Trap* marks a departure from both series, as does another stand-alone novel, *The Sleeping and the Dead* (October 2001). Ann's film for Border TV, *Catching Birds*, won a Television Society award. She is currently involved in reader development programmes, including a writer-in-residence scheme in two northern prisons, and has recently taken on the role of bookings secretary for Murder Squad.

 **Martin Edwards** is the author of seven crime novels featuring Liverpool solicitor Harry Devlin, and the series is optioned for TV. The first, *All the Lonely People*, was shortlisted for the John Creasey Memorial Dagger for the best first crime novel in 1991. Subsequent titles include *Suspicious Minds, Eve of Destruction* and *The First Cut Is the Deepest.*
Martin has edited ten crime fiction anthologies, and his own collected short fiction, *Where Do You Find Your Ideas? and other crime stories*, appeared in 2001. Martin is head of employment law at Liverpool solicitors Mace & Jones.

 **Margaret Murphy**, described as 'one of our most talented new crime writers', explores the psychology of violent criminals and the isolation experienced by victims of crime in her novels. Her first, *Goodnight My Angel,* was shortlisted for the 'First Blood' award for debut crime fiction, and her fourth, *Past Reason*, has been optioned for TV adaptation. The paperback of *Dying Embers*, 'a shocking portrait of the abuse of power' (*The Big Issue*), came out in September 2001, and her new novel, *Darkness Falls,* will be published by Hodder & Stoughton in April 2002. Margaret is the founder of Murder Squad.

 **Stuart Pawson** began writing seriously after a career as an engineer. The first novel in his series featuring Detective Inspector Charlie Priest, *The Picasso Scam,* was well received, and the second, *The Mushroom Man,* was described as 'actually better than his excellent debut'. Stuart's trademark as a writer is the dry humour with which Charlie Priest lightens the squalor of his daily work. Stuart's latest book, *Chill Factor*, is the seventh in this series.

 **Cath Staincliffe** launched her series of private-eye novels set in Manchester, where she now lives, with *Looking for Trouble.* Shortlisted for the CWA's John Creasey Memorial Dagger for best first novel and serialised on *Woman's Hour* on BBC Radio 4, this introduced Sal Kilkenny, a single parent struggling to juggle home and her work as an investigator. Since then, Cath has written four more Sal Kilkenny mysteries, the latest being *Stone Cold Red Hot.*